THE WORLD'S FINEST ASSASSIN

Gets Reincarnated in Another World as an Aristocrat

Contents

The World's Finest Assassin
Gets Reincarnated in Another World as an Aristocrat

"What do you think? I thought I would treat you to a look at me in this camisole. Isn't it cute?"

THE WORLD'S FINEST ASSASSIN

Gets Reincarnated in Another World as an Aristocrat

7

Rui Tsukiyo

Illustration by Reia

YEN
ON

New York

The World's Finest Assassin Gets Reincarnated in Another World as an Aristocrat, Vol. 7
Rui Tsukiyo

Translation by Luke Hutton
Cover art by Reia

SEKAI SAIKO NO ANSATSUSHA, ISEKAI KIZOKU NI TENSEI SURU Vol. 7
©Rui Tsukiyo, Reia 2022
First published in Japan in 2022 by KADOKAWA CORPORATION, Tokyo.
English translation rights arranged with KADOKAWA CORPORATION, Tokyo through TUTTLE-MORI AGENCY, INC., Tokyo.

English translation © 2023 by Yen Press, LLC

Yen On
150 West 30th Street, 19th Floor
New York, NY 10001

Visit us at yenpress.com
facebook.com/yenpress
twitter.com/yenpress
yenpress.tumblr.com
instagram.com/yenpress

First Yen On Edition: July 2023
Edited by Yen On Editorial: Jordan Blanco
Designed by Yen Press Design: Andy Swist

Yen On is an imprint of Yen Press, LLC.
The Yen On name and logo are trademarks of Yen Press, LLC.

Library of Congress Cataloging-in-Publication Data
Names: Tsukiyo, Rui, author. | Reia, 1990– illustrator.
Title: The world's finest assassin gets reincarnated in another world / Rui Tsukiyo; illustration by Reia.
Other titles: Sekai saikou no ansatsusha, isekai kizoku ni tensei suru. English
Description: First Yen On edition. | New York: Yen On, 2020–
Identifiers: LCCN 2020043584 | ISBN 9781975312411 (v. 1; trade paperback) |
    ISBN 9781975312435 (v. 2; trade paperback) | ISBN 9781975333355 (v. 3; trade paperback) |
    ISBN 9781975334574 (v. 4; trade paperback) | ISBN 9781975334659 (v. 5; trade paperback) |
    ISBN 9781975343323 (v. 6; trade paperback) | ISBN 9781975367220 (v. 7; trade paperback)
Subjects: LCSH: Assassins—Fiction. | GSAFD: Fantasy fiction.
Classification: LCC PL876.S858 S4513 2020 | DDC 895.6/36—dc23
LC record available at https://lccn.loc.gov/2020043584

ISBNs: 978-1-9753-6722-0 (paperback)
       978-1-9753-6723-7 (ebook)

10 9 8 7 6 5 4 3 2 1

LSC-C

Printed in the United States of America

We were staying at an inn in the holy city, the headquarters of the world's largest religion, Alamism. It wasn't exactly by choice—the church held us here to prevent us from leaving the city.

I was sitting on my bed and reading some documents. Three days had passed since I'd killed the demon that took the place of the hierarch to control the Alamite Church. I wanted to return to the academy immediately but wasn't allowed. The reason was simple—if word got out that the hierarch had been a demon in disguise, the scandal would shake Alamism to its core.

Is this really enough to cover up this incident? I wondered. Yesterday, the church finally shared with me their plan to keep the scandal under wraps. They wanted to make me into a savior and distract the people with tales of my valor. *Getting too famous is less than ideal as a noble assassin... But the church is determined. Who's gonna believe this story, anyway?*

The documents I read outlined their fabricated story. According to their version of events, the high priests were aware that the demon had taken the hierarch's place. However, the demon's strength prevented the church from taking action—if they said anything, the demon would have revealed his true identity and slaughtered everyone in the holy city. Thus, the priests feigned ignorance and summoned Lugh Tuatha Dé, a Holy Knight, to the holy city as a supposed traitor. Then, with the support of the high priests, Lugh Tuatha Dé joined forces with the Alam Karla, the oracle of the goddess, and defeated the demon.

I credit their imagination, I thought. It allowed the church's management to claim that all their wrongdoing, including publicly branding me a traitor of the goddess, had been in the interest of eliminating the demon. To fool your enemy, you must first fool your friends... That was their excuse. This version of events would lead the public to think of the church's management as heroes rather than incompetent fools strung along by the demon.

The church needed my cooperation to make this story into reality. It wouldn't be believable otherwise. *They nearly executed me as an enemy of the goddess. I want nothing more than to tell them to piss off.* However, I had no choice but to cooperate. A great many people relied on their faith in Alamism, and the world would fall into chaos if the religion crumbled. That was true in my home country of Alvan as well.

The church needed to maintain its dignity. Cooperating with its story was in Alvan's best interest. As an Alvanian noble, I had to prioritize the kingdom over my personal feelings. *Worst-case scenario, the church could have tried to save face by fabricating a crime and executing me. This is preferable.*

The leaders of the Alamite Church were obsessed with appearances, but I had to admire their pragmatism. Their incredible sense for management was what allowed them to grow Alamism into the world's largest religion. Such a large-scale organization could not operate on faith alone. Plus, this story wasn't so bad for me. Regardless of its authenticity, it would erase any notion that I was an enemy of the church.

"Hey, Lugh!"

Hearing my name jerked me out of my thoughts, and I sat up on the bed.

"Is it really okay for us to stay here? I'm starting to feel kind of intimidated."

The person speaking to me was a petite girl who was at once intelligent and cute. She was fiddling with her distinct silver hair. Her name was Dia. She was my little sister, according to the family register, but in reality, she was my magic teacher and a romantic partner.

"Is this inn really such a big deal? It doesn't seem luxurious to me."

The room's other occupant was an adorable young girl with blond hair and a sizable chest that attracted male gazes. She was Tarte, my personal retainer and assassination assistant.

"Are you serious, Tarte? Of course it's a big deal. A never-ending stream of nobles and merchants spend an exorbitant amount of money just to stay here," Dia said.

"Huh?! Is that true?! I can't see why. The rooms aren't that nice, and the food is lacking," Tarte responded.

As Tarte claimed, our room wasn't particularly lavish. The food was only better than average, and the service was ordinary. The price, however, was out of this world.

"I suppose I've yet to teach you much about religion, Tarte... Sorry, I should've gotten to that already. It's essential knowledge for a personal retainer. I'll take this opportunity to educate you," I said.

It was Tarte's job as my personal retainer to accompany and serve me in front of guests. Besides possessing the skills of a servant, personal retainers needed the finest etiquette to avoid embarrass-ing their master and sufficient social aptitude and education to keep up with the discussions of the aristocracy. Retainer positions were typically assumed by decently educated individuals from good families after they'd served for three years doing the lowest servant work out of sight from guests, followed by another three years aiding a top attendant. That was the ideal path to becoming a personal retainer.

Tarte didn't receive a decent education as a child, and although she worked hard, two years was not enough time to acquire all the skills and knowledge necessary of an assassin's assistant and personal retainer. I'd narrowed her focus to the culture she would come across most often in the aristocratic world, knowing she could make up for whatever knowledge she lacked with her tremendous effort, so I'd only lightly touched on religion.

"Don't apologize, Lord Lugh. It's my own fault for slacking on my studies," Tarte responded hurriedly. She was always debasing herself. I'd let it slide until now, understanding that humility was a part of her personality, but it was a bad habit she needed to fix.

"You're too quick to apologize, Tarte. It's a bad habit. Always assuming you've done wrong causes you to lose sight of the truth and isn't helpful. People improve by learning from their mistakes... I'll never grow if you always put the blame on yourself, and as my student, you won't grow, either."

"I-I'm sorry," Tarte said.

She was apologizing again. Fixing this bad habit wouldn't be easy. I racked my brains for how to handle this, and Dia spoke up.

"You need to work on that, Tarte. It's part of a servant's duty to correct their master. That's especially true for a personal retainer. It'll be in Lugh's best interest."

"Yes, you're right. Sor—er, I'll do my best."

"That's more like it."

Dia nodded. Her petite stature made her look childish, but she was a smart and caring person. She'd acted like an older sister toward me from the day we met, and it didn't seem like that was ever going to change. Lately, her stock phrase had changed from "your big sister knows best" to "your first wife knows best," and her sisterly attentions had expanded to include Tarte and Maha.

Perhaps it was best to leave this matter to her.

"I'm counting on you, Tarte. You're the best personal retainer there is," I said.

"My lord is counting on me... I—I will devote myself to improving!" Tarte declared, clenching her fists. It looked like I had nothing to worry about.

I needed to adjust my mindset, too. Tarte was more than an impromptu servant—she was perfectly capable of becoming a truly elite retainer. I needed to gradually teach her the things I'd omitted from her education.

"Okay, I'll start by explaining what makes this building special. It's called the House of the Divine, and it's one of the most revered sites of the holy city. Only guests of the gods are allowed inside. The simple act of staying here gives one the prestige of being recognized as a special person by the Alamite Church. Many guests claim they were blessed by the goddess."

"Oh, I see. But Lady Dia said that a room costs a lot. No one finds it weird that you can buy a blessing with money?"

That was a sharp observation. I didn't expect Tarte to think of that. Her purity was likely what allowed her to see the true nature of this place.

"If major nobles spend a great amount of money to stay here and boast about it afterward, that's enough to convince the rest of aristocratic society that it's something worth doing. Others will follow suit to gain the honor for themselves." Tarte nodded to show she understood me. "Also, it's not necessarily wrong to be proud of the money one spends here."

"What do you mean?"

"The Alamite Church performs philanthropic work worldwide. Things like feeding the hungry and managing orphanages. Donations enable those endeavors. In a roundabout way, the high room price saves lives. The more people stay here, the better the world."

Some people questioned whether spending money was really enough to win divine favor, but the funds went to a good cause. The vast sums donated on the whims of the rich saved hundreds of times as many lives as the poor did with volunteer work.

"Oh, that makes sense! So that's how spending money earns the goddess's approval! Huh? Do you not agree, Lady Dia?" Tarte asked.

"Sounds like a real stretch to me," Dia replied.

"The church really is saving many lives using that money. On that point, they deserve nothing but praise," I argued.

I truly applauded the church for constructing this system. The rich satisfied their vanity, and the poor benefited. I couldn't imagine a better win-win situation... Except for the rumor that 70 percent of the donations disappeared into the pockets of the church's leaders. Even then, the remaining 30 percent made the world a better place.

Religious leaders often attracted enmity. I assassinated many of them in my past life, and from what I learned researching those targets, 30 percent of donations going to philanthropic work was actually quite good.

By comparison, one religion in my previous world spent 80

percent of its donations on wide-reaching commercials. The remainder was spent primarily on publicity to propagate the faith's teachings. The religion collected donations equivalent to the revenue of a major company and didn't use it to save anyone.

"I know what it is like to be poor. When you're hungry and near death, it doesn't matter how your food is prepared... You'll take anything to fill your stomach," Tarte said.

Those words meant a lot coming from Tarte, who was kicked out of her village to reduce the number of mouths to feed.

"Sorry, Tarte. You're right. I didn't consider the feelings of those helped," Dia apologized.

"Alamism is extraordinary for creating a system that aids people with the indulgences of the wealthy. That's why, under normal circumstances, only the rich can stay here. All guests receive a sacred gift as proof of their visit," I said.

"What kind of gift?" asked Tarte.

"A necklace with a gem blessed by an Alamite priest. You see people flaunting them at noble parties all the time."

The necklaces were finely crafted, but the gems were crude. Major nobles and merchants regularly displayed the cheap accessories as though they were things to be proud of. Religion was truly amusing.

"Why do they give out necklaces?"

"It would be difficult for noble guests to boast about a visit here otherwise. It also prevents people from lying about staying. Anyone can *claim* to visit the House of the Divine, but no will believe them without a necklace. You have to pay to receive the real thing."

"It sounds like a business."

"Religious leaders have a much stronger sense for business than your average merchant. The larger the faith, the more likely that is to be true. After all, they need vast sums of money to expand their church, tough negotiating skills to gain all the rights they want in multiple countries, and the ability to curry favor and capture the hearts of powerful individuals. Those are all skills required of elite merchants."

Religious activity couldn't survive on teaching doctrine and moving hearts. There was a direct correlation between a faith's size and its ability to generate revenue.

"Oh, Lugh. I just thought of something. I'll bet we could earn a ton of money making and selling a bunch of those necklaces," Dia suggested.

"That's a bad idea, Lady Dia. We'd be punished," Tarte chided.

"Really? I'm sure the goddess has more important things to worry about."

I thought about the goddess that Alamism revered. She claimed that merely speaking to me consumed resources used to maintain the world, and thus rarely showed herself. There was no way she'd punish everyone who infringed on the profit of her religion. It wouldn't be worth the resources. However...

"Tarte's right. Anyone who makes goods related to Alamism without permission is branded an enemy of the divine. This gem is carved with the holy symbol of the faith, and you're finished if you use that without permission. It means the death penalty in any country where Alamism is the national religion... Some idiots actually tried that in the past," I explained.

"Gods are surprisingly materialistic," Dia commented.

"Like I said, the larger the religion, the better its leaders are at business. They can also get away with anything as long as they say it's 'for the gods.' You're asking for it if you pick a fight with them."

A businessperson couldn't permit anyone to infringe on their profit.

"Thank you very much, my lord. I feel like I learned a lot. I will take care of the necklaces we receive... They will be a perfect source of money should we ever need to flee!" Tarte exclaimed.

Dia and Tarte looked at each other and laughed.

"Yeah, they would be perfect for that," I said.

"Totally. They're small and would net us a ton of money," Dia agreed.

Working as assassins was dangerous. The royal family would cut ties with us at the first sign of any collusion. For that reason, we'd hidden wealth throughout Alvan and abroad and prepared safe houses and fake identities for ourselves.

However, it might still be difficult to reach safety when we needed to escape. We could end up with someone right on our tail, giving us no time to collect our money. The holy necklaces were convenient because we could wear them at all times and easily sell them for a high price. The church wouldn't be able to identify who peddled the necklaces, given that there were so many in circulation. I couldn't think of better assets for a tight situation.

It was the same reason gangsters wore Rolexes. They weren't for show—the watches were easy to carry and could be sold quickly for a good sum.

"I'm impressed you came up with that idea, Tarte... You've really grown," I said.

"Um, did I say something weird?" she responded.

"No, I'm praising you."

One of the problems caused by Tarte's upbringing was her

inability to act unless instructed. She struggled to think for her-self. Her assessment of the situation and subsequent suggestion were signs she was conquering that weakness.

Tarte mistook my praise for teasing and sulked. I laughed at her response, and that caused her to sulk more. While I thought of how to clear up the misunderstanding, someone knocked on the door—an Alamite deacon assigned to look after us.

"Sir Tuatha Dé, the cardinals have summoned you."

Cardinals ranked just below the hierarch in the Alamite Church's echelons.

"I'll leave right away. Dia, Tarte, let's go out to eat when I get back. I'm sure you're grateful for the food the House of the Divine has provided us, but it's rather lacking. I'm ready for a good meal," I said.

"That sounds nice. We get nothing but bland-tasting vegeta-bles here. I want some salted meat," Dia replied.

"I agree. We don't get enough food here," Tarte said.

The meeting with the cardinals was going to be a pain. Hav-ing dinner with Dia and Tarte to look forward to would help me get through it.

Chapter 1 | The Assassin Accepts a Lie

I headed for the cathedral, where I was to meet the cardinals. It was located in the center of the holy city and was one of the symbols of Alamism. Just setting foot inside this place was something you could brag about for the rest of your life, as was the case with the House of the Divine, too.

Tourists were not allowed inside the cathedral. They could only observe it from afar or offer their prayers in one of the many other churches in the city. Many dreamed of earning the privilege to enter the cathedral by doing good in the world.

A tall and polite young deacon guided me. "Sir Tuatha Dé, you will speak with the cardinals. Please do your best to avoid offending them," he cautioned.

"I understand," I responded with a smile.

Hierarch was the top position in the Alamite Church, followed by the cardinals, patriarchs, archbishops, bishops, priests, and deacons. Priests and deacons worked as ministers for an individual church, bishops governed all the churches in a town, and the higher positions were executives who made decisions for the entire Alamite Church.

The Alam Karla was not a part of the church's hierarchy, just a symbol with no real power.

The cardinals who summoned me were second only to the

hierarch. They were people I'd ordinarily never speak with. I'd always held a decent amount of respect for them, but my opinion dropped considerably after they publicly branded me a criminal.

I'm an Alvanian noble, though. I have to behave myself.

I was representing the Alvanian Kingdom in this meeting. I'd heard that Alvan had sent a negotiator qualified for this occasion, but I'd yet to meet them. This discussion was going to influence the fate of our nation—no one wanted to entrust that to a child like me. I would've preferred to meet the negotiator and learn about the kingdom's wants beforehand, but it sounded as though they'd arrived only just before the discussion.

All I had to do was figure out what this negotiator wanted and align my words accordingly. It was better not to make any independent decisions, no matter what the cardinals asked of me. *If there were an instructor with me.* That would have helped me relax. Unfortunately, the instructors were told they weren't qualified to enter the cathedral.

That was probably a calculated choice. Sure, the claim that teachers weren't qualified was plausible, but I saw what the cardinals were up to. They figured that winning over a child would be easy, no matter how strong I was, and they wanted to get me as close to alone as they could. They'd likely pay more attention to me than the negotiator, hoping to wring out accidental promises from me.

Facing the cardinals would be tough. Large religious organizations were essentially collectives of elite merchants. It was impossible to climb to the top of such an organization without political skill, an intelligence network, connections, and money; virtue and faith had nothing to do with it. You needed to be a monster to become a cardinal.

A familiar face waited for me in the hallway.

"Hello, Lugh. Thank you for your service in the holy city. You can relax now that I'm here."

The man addressing me was inhumanly handsome. He wore a splendid purple outfit few could hope to pull off so well. It matched the color of his hair. He was the head of a noble family that had spent hundreds of years performing selective breeding to create the ultimate humans. It was the duke of House Romalung, patriarch of one of the four major dukedoms.

"It is nice to see you again, Duke Romalung," I responded.

"Same to you. I'm glad to see you're well after your latest ordeal. I wouldn't be able to face Baron Tuatha Dé if anything happened to you."

"If that's how you feel, you should have done something to help me escape execution. Your information network surely knew of the church's plans before I was summoned here."

I'd been invited on the pretense of commendation for slaying demons, but the real intent was to execute me for misappropriating the goddess's name. My head was nearly cut off. I could have died.

"Yes, we knew. But this is you we're talking about. You could've contacted me through Nevan, but you didn't. Instead, you marched to your trial knowing it was a trap... I believed you'd escape without my help, and that's precisely what you did."

I couldn't believe my ears. Constructing my telecommunications network cost me as much as purchasing a small nation, but it was worth it to gather information at unprecedented speeds for a world that relied on physical letters. Somehow, Duke Romalung acquired the same amount of information as I did, without that advantage. I definitely didn't want to make an enemy of him. I was glad the duke was an ally in the upcoming meeting. No one was better equipped for this situation.

"I'm glad the kingdom sent you. I can follow your lead," I said.

"Yes, please do. You're brilliant, but you're a man of action. You're not ready for politics," the duke responded.

He spoke the truth. I was adept at gathering information, using my intelligence network, and analyzing situations, and I could grasp the current situation, but only those entrenched in government could properly speak on political matters. Something I judged as the right course of action could be seen as the wrong move by someone with knowledge of the bigger picture.

"You're right. I'll just do my best not to get in your way during the meeting."

"I knew you were special. I hope you will consider impregnating Nevan. I know your seed will produce the greatest Romalung to ever live. We'd finally achieve our family's long-held ambition of creating humanity's ultimate masterpiece."

"Let's table that discussion for now."

We walked to the conference room where the cardinals waited. What were they going to throw at me?

I looked around the conference room. The church called it something different, but the deacon guiding me thought that title would be easiest for us to understand. The space was impressive.

It's designed to influence the minds of those who enter.

Ninety percent of the information processed by the human

brain is visual. This means you could influence a person's feelings by manipulating what they saw. This room was constructed perfectly to inspire awe in those who entered. That was evident from the desk alone. Its shape, placement, and the intensity and color of the light illuminating it had all been meticulously planned.

As far as I was aware, psychology didn't exist in this world. This layout must have been the result of trial and error. The tenacity of working to this end was admirable. It was clear that the Alamite Church didn't become the world's most prevalent religion simply because its leaders had a girl who could hear the goddess's voice; the religion grew because its leaders were clever.

Seven people sat on the church's side of the table. Each one was a cardinal who managed the churches in multiple countries and had the power to manipulate believers under their jurisdiction.

The Alvanian Kingdom was a major power, but from the church's perspective, Duke Romalung and I were nobles from one of many nations. The cardinals' eyes and attitudes unmistakably communicated a feeling of superiority.

"Greetings, Sir Tuatha Dé. You have served us most splendidly."

I understood that the cardinals supremely outranked me, but I was amazed they still remained haughty after screwing up so badly during the Puppeteer demon incident.

"Thank you for your kind words." I kept my thoughts about their attitude to myself and sat down after the deacon motioned for me to do so.

"Thank you as well for coming all this way, Duke Romalung. You may be seated."

Duke Romalung smiled and obeyed without a word.

"Let us discuss the demon attack. Anyone ignorant of the

true events will think this incident to be the fault of the Alamite Church. This is despite our efforts to fool even those closest to us in an effort to eliminate the demon that supplanted the hierarch. That misunderstanding would be most deplorable."

The cardinals all looked at me. The message was loud and clear. They weren't asking me to align my story with theirs—they were insisting that their version was the truth. The difference was subtle, but critical. Asking me not to lie but to make that falsehood the truth changed everything.

How should I answer?

Duke Romalung simply smiled and signaled for me to be silent. Alvanian nobles shared a set of unique signals that came in handy for communicating information quickly and wordlessly while abroad.

I see. That's what we're doing. I smiled and did as Duke Romalung requested. The cardinals' surly faces twitched.

"As you are aware, we knew the hierarch was possessed by a demon. If we said anything, however, the demon would have revealed himself and rained fire upon the holy city... Only the hero or a Holy Knight could defeat him. Openly asking for help would have also led the demon to destroy the city. We had no choice but to summon you as a criminal to be executed. We knew the demon would welcome your execution, as you'd killed several of his brethren already. Your capture would allow him to eliminate a threat."

The duke was still signaling me to remain quiet, and I acquiesced.

"Word of your demon-killing exploits gave us a very high opinion of you. It wounded us to brand you a criminal, even though it was a temporary measure. Still, it was the only way to fool the demon!"

There was real passion in their acting. I expected nothing less of cardinals—they all knew how to appeal to the heart. They'd likely convinced themselves to the point that they weren't aware they were lying.

"You more than lived up to our expectations. I knew we were right to name you a saint! We must let the world know you are the eighth saint to ever live. The truth of this incident must be made clear first, however. Can we count on your cooperation?"

They dangled bait before me while presenting their lie as truth. Becoming a saint wouldn't grant me any direct authority, but I would be able to get away with anything in countries where Alamism was the official religion. I'd be treated as a god. That was worth more than all the money in the world. My words would carry the power of a king's. I wasn't interested, though. That sort of power only brought disaster and trouble.

I watched Duke Romalung from the corner of my vision without moving my eyes. He gave me a new sign commanding me to agree.

"I understand. I will follow your orders," I said.

"We're glad to see you understand. We will make a spectacular show of your canonization as a saint. There shall be a grand festival with nobles from across the continent, members of the church, and major businesspeople. It will be held in a week, and we shall do our best to make yours a celebration of unprecedented glory."

How shameless. They were clearly doing this for the church, not for me. The spectacle was a distraction to bury the scandal and to help their version of events pass unquestioned. This plan would likely succeed; the people wanted the demons gone, and a demon-killer becoming a saint would stoke tremendous joy.

"We have prepared a speech for you since you lack experience in such matters. Please read this verbatim at your ceremony."

The deacon handed me a thick bundle of papers. A quick scan revealed it was quite thorough. It was written in the church's best interest, of course, but none of it put me at a disadvantage.

"This concludes the meeting. Thank you for your cooperation."

How abrupt.

Duke Romalung raised his hand just as I thought that. "The Alvanian Kingdom agrees with Lugh's decision to cooperate. I cannot allow you to have his support for free, however. He is taking a risk by spreading your lies, so I expect appropriate compensation."

He pulled documents out of a bag and distributed them to everyone present. I looked them over and nearly laughed. The duke was really toeing the line. The paper outlined conditions beneficial to the Alvanian Kingdom that the church had the power to grant. The cardinals would be very reluctant to approve these demands… But given the risk of their predicament, they had to agree. Duke Romalung played this to perfection.

"What do you mean by 'lies'?"

"Exactly what I said. The demon had you all dancing on his strings. Lugh's quick wit allowed you all to escape with your positions intact. I am fine with telling your story publicly, but the truth must remain the truth between Alvan and the church."

Duke Romalung's smile was impossibly beautiful, but looking at it gave me the chilling sense that he could see into the soul.

"We have told no lies. What we say is the truth."

"You've all been careless. I know that every one of you secretly tried to gain favor with the hierarch while the demon had you under his thumb. Your hunger for glory caused you to leave behind plenty of evidence that disproves your story. Lots of people from other countries have noticed this as well."

Duke Romalung produced more papers, and more surprises. These documents were based on information collected by Natural You's information network. And I could tell from the files' presentation that Maha wrote them.

Did Nevan tell her father about the telecommunications network and that Maha managed it? No, there's no way. Nevan wasn't that kind of person. I was confident she'd keep that secret, as promised. However, that suggested Duke Romalung learned of the telecommunications network and traced its management back to Maha on his own.

My poker face felt ready to crack. I knew the duke was a monster, but this was beyond reason. The cardinals shared my sentiment, turning pale when they read the documents.

Duke Romalung refused to let up, saying, "I take it you realize how bad it would be for you if this information were made public? Especially the multiple assassination attempts on the Alam Karla after Lugh rescued her. You did a poor job covering your tracks in your efforts to earn favor with the hierarch. Tracing the orders back to you all was simple. Alamism may be the most influential religion in the world, but some countries will be glad to be rid of it. You don't want this information to get out."

"Such insolence! Do you really think a noble representing a single kingdom can threaten us?! We could crush Alvan in three days if we so wished!"

The cardinals' saintly skin had been torn off to reveal them for what they were—small men obsessed with power. The problem was, they genuinely could destroy Alvan. Most major countries on the continent would attack if the church gave the command.

"You're missing my point. I'm saying the Alvanian Kingdom will support you. We'll help spread your lie and erase the evidence you left behind. I'm confident that your story will collapse without our assistance, leaks or no leaks. Acknowledge the lie for what it is."

Alvan wanted the cardinals to recognize the lie to put the church in its debt. The kingdom couldn't accomplish this by agreeing to propagate the "truth," but agreeing to spread a lie carried a sizable risk, giving Alvan something it could hold over the church. The value of that was immeasurable.

This was a dangerous negotiation. Push the cardinals too far and they'd decide that Alvan needed to be destroyed. Duke Romalung was treading a tightrope. He was confident he could pull it off, but this was beyond my capabilities.

I could probably have pushed the cardinals to this point. After all, it was my subordinate, Maha, who had gathered the information the duke presented. However, I lacked the courage to take on this kind of challenge, and I wouldn't have any confidence in success.

After a long silence, one of the cardinals forced himself to speak through a dry throat.

"Very well. We accept your conditions. Please cooperate and spread our sequence of events."

The cardinals were too stubborn to admit their story was false. Still, Duke Romalung won this meeting. He'd successfully crossed the tightrope.

"Thank you very much. Let us work together for the prosperity of the Alamite Church and the Alvanian Kingdom." The duke grinned.

Geez, he's unbelievable. I had to speak with him later. I needed to know how he intended to use his knowledge of Maha.

Duke Romalung and I left the cathedral and went to a favorite restaurant of his. I wanted to return to the inn for dinner to keep my promise to Dia and Tarte, but I couldn't refuse an invitation from the head of one of the four major dukedoms. Plus, I needed to discern his intentions for Maha.

The restaurant Duke Romalung led me to was a perfectly normal café, except for its private rooms.

"The owner of this establishment is from Alvan. He's always been willing to help me out," Duke Romalung said. He probably came here for work often. It was perfect for private conversation.

A patron entered the restaurant after us and complained furiously when he was told there were no tables available.

"He'll even turn customers away for you. Must be why you chose this place," I remarked.

"Precisely. I would rather our discussion not be overheard."

The person who made a fuss had tailed us from the cathedral. He was almost certainly an Alamite Church agent. The cardinals didn't fully trust us. The man could have forced his way in by claiming affiliation with the church, but he had to keep his identity secret.

"Hello, Sir Lugh. It's a pleasure to see you."

"I am so sorry for the trouble I have caused you."

Two people were waiting in the private room. I'd expected one, but not the other.

The first was Nevan, Duke Romalung's daughter, the family masterpiece. The other was the Alam Karla, the living symbol of Alamism. She looked no different from an ordinary girl without the makeup and wig she wore to resemble the goddess.

"I heard that House Romalung is safeguarding the Alam Karla," I said.

"Technically, the Alvanian embassy has taken her into custody," Nevan replied.

I saved the Alam Karla's life from assassins. She would return to her position after a thorough investigation confirmed she wouldn't be in danger. That's what the Alvanian Kingdom proposed. I couldn't imagine how anyone got the church to agree. Undoubtedly, it involved a lot of work behind the scenes.

"I'm glad to see you are well, Your Holiness," I greeted her.

"And I am glad you are unhurt, Sir Lugh," the Alam Karla answered.

I'd worried for the Alam Karla, but Nevan was doing a good job taking care of her.

"I'm hurt. Were you not even a little concerned for me?" Nevan asked.

"You can take care of yourself, Nevan," I responded.

Nevan was undoubtedly the strongest person I'd met in my age range. She was clever, physically gifted...and smart. I didn't mean that she was great at math or possessed a strong memory. Nevan was resourceful and always chose the best course of action.

Perfection in one so young was frightening. I had to wonder if she was reincarnated like I was.

I turned to Duke Romalung. "So why did you invite these two?"

"Would you believe me if I told you that it's to support my daughter's love life?"

He played that off as a joke, but I bet he was more than half serious. Duke Romalung's goal was to produce the ultimate humans. He'd devoted himself to finding superior blood. And I knew he and his daughter thought highly of me.

"I can't imagine that's the only reason."

"You're right. I want to ask something of the Alam Karla, and given the nature of the request, I thought it would be best to have you here. My daughter is present as the Alam Karla's bodyguard."

Nevan also served as a body double for the princess of the Alvanian Kingdom. That was how she met the Alam Karla and built a friendship with her, and how she learned of the oracle's predicament before anyone else. No one was more qualified to safeguard the Alam Karla.

"My gratitude knows no bounds, Sir Lugh... You're also the only person in the world who shares my gift, so I will offer my help with whatever you need," the Alam Karla said.

Duke Romalung grinned. "Your 'gift'? Are you referring to your ability to hear the goddess's voice? Color me surprised. I thought you made that up to spread the demon-killing formula you created, Lugh."

Scarily enough, he was actually right. The goddess did speak to me, but she had nothing to do with Demonkiller. I claimed the goddess gave the spell to me because it was a convenient excuse.

"I do hear the goddess's voice," I replied.

Nevan smiled. "I have no doubt that's true. Whether or not

you've shared everything the goddess has told you, or if all the words you've attributed to her genuinely came from her mouth, is a different matter."

Nevan was as sharp as her father. She saw through my misleading statement.

"All I can say is that I convey the goddess's words. More pressingly, what do you require of the Alam Karla, Duke Romalung?" I inquired.

"Ah, yes. Your Holiness. I have a request for you as a duke of the Alvanian Kingdom and as a friend of Lugh's. I want you to affirm anything and everything Lugh says. Depending on how things play out, we could make an enemy of the Alamite Church. As long as you side with us, however, justice will remain with Lugh."

The Alam Karla was a symbol with no real power. There was no need for the girl who filled the position to be a true oracle; the church would be glad to have a puppet who spoke lies that benefited their organization.

The Alam Karla had nearly been replaced the other day, but the attempt ended up strengthening the current one's position. Everyone knew the demon had prepared a fake Alam Karla, making it difficult for the church to repeat the same stunt on its own. Now no one would believe a new Alam Karla was born days after the current one's disappearance. The church couldn't replace her. Thus, her friendship was an enormous weapon for us.

"Of course. I promise I'll do just that."

The Alam Karla squeezed my hands tight, looked me straight in the eye, and nodded. Duke Romalung smiled bitterly.

"You're a real lady-killer, Lugh. First my daughter falls for you, and now the oracle of the Alamite Church."

"N-no, I do not think of Sir Lugh that way. He saved my life. I am grateful to him, and I respect him." The Alam Karla was quick to refuse Duke Romalung's claim, but she was obviously lying.

Given her position, she presumably lacked experience with romance. I decided to help her out.

"Do not insult Her Holiness, Duke Romalung. My social standing is hardly worthy of hers."

A mixed expression of relief and disappointment showed on the Alam Karla's face. I pretended not to notice. I'd never be able to return her affection, and I wanted to avoid rejecting and hurting her, which risked losing her cooperation. Surely, Duke Romalung was aware of that possibility. Why was he going out of his way to instigate?

"Thank goodness. That's one less rival to worry about. I am serious about you, Lugh. Please consider my offer of marriage," Nevan said.

"My answer has not changed since we last spoke," I responded bluntly.

"How cold."

It wasn't a bad proposal. I suspected that Nevan didn't harbor romantic feelings for me and simply wanted my superior blood. I'd be free once she was pregnant, and any compensation I received would mean greater prosperity for the Tuatha Dé domain. Still, I had no intention to accept. My heart only had room for Dia, Tarte, and Maha.

"That concludes my business. Let's enjoy some tea and sweets."

Duke Romalung snapped his fingers, and waiters carrying drinks and snacks entered the room. I'd seen these people before, in House Romalung's castle.

He said the café's owner is from Alvan... House Romalung runs this place.

"That sounds wonderful. Is that agreeable for you, Sir Lugh?" Nevan asked.

"Naturally. I have some questions, though."

I needed to learn how the duke got ahold of Maha's documents.

"Ask away. This is about Maha, yes? She's a good girl. Were Nevan a boy, I'd want her for House Romalung," the duke said.

He really did know about Maha.

"How did you learn that Maha is the center of my information network?"

I'd assumed the duke knew about my information network, but I never expected him to trace it to its manager.

"I suppose it was because of how she worries over you. She's normally untraceable, but the moment you wind up in danger she gets so desperate to save you that she fails to cover her tracks... My agents don't miss something like that. That's the only reason we found her. You have nothing to worry about—none but House Romalung could notice her mistakes."

Easy for him to say. Maha definitely pushed herself hard for my sake, but she never left evidence. What constituted as "tracks" differed for Duke Romalung, though. He could pick up on the most trivial details.

"What are you going to do now that you know about her? Do you have a demand for me?"

Maha was irreplaceable. She was the heart of my funds and information, and I would pay anything to protect her.

"No. I don't intend to hold this over you. Doing anything to torment and limit you harms the kingdom. Producing the ultimate humans is my family's top priority, but we remain aware of our duty as Alvanian nobles. You have nothing to fear." That Duke Romalung demanded nothing actually frightened me more. "Oh, right. Since you're asking, I do have one request."

"...What is it?"

"I would like permission to use your so-called telecommunications network when I have need of it. Just once. You've built something incredible. I could never have assembled documents like those I presented at the meeting. Maha has my gratitude. Negotiation would have been impossible if not for her."

His request sounded like nothing, but it was actually quite a big ask.

"Very well. I'll let you know how to contact the intelligence agents I have stationed in each city."

Allowing the duke to use the telecommunications network at any time meant sharing information on the agents I kept deployed in each city. After all, I definitely couldn't reveal the locations of the switchboards or the terminals connected to them. There was no option but to give up the people who handled the terminals.

"My apologies for imposing," the duke said.

"Don't worry about it. Take care when using the telecommunications network, though. You should assume that I will hear anything you say," I warned.

"Yes, I've heard that about the system already."

That warning was a lie. One Maha had apparently been spreading, too. Changing the channel restricted who heard a message sent through the network, but I kept that feature hidden.

Duke Romalung sighed. "I think it's a waste to keep your invention secret. It will change the world."

"Absolutely. The need to relay information through physical parcels is restricting. It hinders the world's development," I agreed.

"Then you should unveil this technology to the public."

I shook my head.

"That would cause an upheaval. Going public with this would flip society upside down, for better or worse. We'd lose the current stability."

Duke Romalung smiled in his usual icy way and clapped exaggeratedly. "I like you more with each meeting. You're a smart man. I'm relieved to hear you say that. If you'd announced an intention to upset the world with that invention... As someone who works to protect our kingdom, I would've had to kill you."

"That's not a joke, is it?"

"Why, of course not. I'm telling you this because I trust that you'll keep the telecommunications network private. If you didn't, I wouldn't hesitate to kill you and ensure no one ever learned what became to you."

I forced a smile and wet my throat with a sip of tea. There was no way I could reciprocate Nevan's feelings. I didn't want this man for a father-in-law. I wouldn't be able to take it. I'd do my best to maintain our current relationship: close enough to remain allies, but not too close.

I returned to my room in the House of the Divine after leaving the café, then went out with Dia and Tarte for an evening of fun. As always, someone was assigned to tail us. I wished the church would assign someone more covert.

"I've never seen you look so tired, Lugh. You're always so composed," Dia said.

"Today was mentally exhausting."

"I'm not surprised. That's what I'd expect from a meeting with the cardinals. I hear they expect people to call them 'Your Holinesses.'"

I hadn't called them that, and I never would as long as I lived.

"The meeting with the cardinals wasn't actually that bad. It's my conversation with Duke Romalung that has me so fatigued… I'll tell you about it later."

Duke Romalung discovering the telecommunications network was something I couldn't keep to myself. Worst case, my intelligence agents would be attacked and stolen. I needed to share this development with the entire team.

"I've never met him, but he sounds intimidating. Like father, like daughter, I suppose," Dia remarked.

"It's scary just imagining what Nevan will be like when she grows up," Tarte added.

They both smiled weakly. Neither one of them seemed comfortable around Nevan.

"Let's forget about that for now. I've been waiting for a chance to have fun and explore the city," I said.

The holy city was considered the most popular place in the world for tourists. Believers traveled from all over, and every company under the sun sought to open a shop here to capitalize on that. The more competitive a city, the higher quality its shops. Adding to the fun, some tourists brought local specialties from their homelands to sell. As a result, storefronts displayed a variety of products from around the world. That gave the holy city an even greater international flavor than Milteu, which had the advantage of a trade harbor. Simple window-shopping was a fun pastime here.

"It's so lively. You'd never think a demon attacked," Dia observed.

"That's because there weren't many victims. Fortunately, this demon preferred to remain hidden rather than attack openly," I replied.

Tarte nodded. "That's a good point. That giant caterpillar would have sunk the entire city."

"Now, that would've been a disaster. Destruction of the holy city would've sent the world into a panic," I said.

The world's largest religion being wiped off the map could only mean immediate chaos.

"Out of the way!"

A horse-drawn carriage raced up from behind, forcing all three of us to dodge. The carriage only barely fit through the narrow street.

Dia scowled. "Geez, they're going to hurt somebody at that speed."

"There are so many carriages in the city today," Tarte remarked.

Few were driving so recklessly, but there definitely were an inordinate number of buggies, and they were all in a hurry.

"Guess that's what happens when the church announces a festival with only a week's warning… Everyone is working furiously to prepare."

Normally, people would spurn such an abrupt celebration. No one would show up, and companies would pass it over because they lacked preparation time. An Alamite Church event was a different matter, though. It was meant to honor a man being canonized as the eighth saint in history, one named a Holy Knight for killing demons. People were desperate not to miss this.

I felt eyes on me. Actually, I sensed that whenever I walked through this city.

"Hey, have people been watching us?" I asked.

"Yep," Dia responded.

"They have," confirmed Tarte.

They sounded very casual.

"Why?"

Dia sniffed. "Because you killed the demon who replaced the hierarch. Duh."

"Well sure, but how do they know that was me?"

A few people saw my face on the scaffold, but they were only a small fraction of those living in this city. Yet it seemed like everyone knew who I was.

In my previous world, information traveled visually through

mediums like television and newspapers, but in this world, it was very rare for a person's face to become widely known. Cameras were still prohibitively expensive and bulky. Most towns didn't have a single one. Plus, picture-taking was a service only offered in shops. Hearsay wasn't enough to be recognized.

"You've been getting summoned to one meeting after another for a few days, but Tarte and I have been free to explore the city."

"What does that have to do it?"

"We know what's happening. Look at this." Dia took my hand and led me to a general store. I saw copies of an expensive book on display through the window. The high price was unusual given the spread of the printing press.

"What?"

The cover had me stunned. It depicted the leader of the cardinals, the Alam Karla…and me. A talented artist had glorified our appearances, but the illustration still captured my likeness well.

"Wow, you're the Holy Knight! Please, come into my store. Would you mind signing one of my prints? I have a large one back here."

The pushy shopkeeper dragged me inside and brought me to a bigger copy of the picture. It was a woodblock print, lower quality than the book covers, but my visage remained unmistakable.

"What is this?" I asked.

"It's a book published by the church called *The Truth Behind the Holy City Demon Incident: To Fool Even the Divine*. It's flying off the shelves. I get a bonus from the church for every copy I sell, too. You can bet I'm gonna push out as many as I can," the shopkeeper explained.

"Can I read a copy?"

"You can if you sign my picture."

I scribbled my name on the large print and opened a book. It gave me an immediate headache. The church's invented story had been embellished to be more romantic and heroic. All the cardinals at the meeting today got a moment to shine, while I was portrayed as rather pompous. I even had a love story with the Alam Karla.

Unsurprisingly, the cardinal on the cover came off the best. He got the key line of the book right before the demon perished: "This was all a performance to catch you unawares, you filthy demon. We will fool even the divine if that is what it takes to protect the gods and their people."

Ah, the title comes from this scene. I remembered this cardinal falling to his knees and wetting himself when the demon made itself known.

"Everyone is reading this, huh?" I mumbled, crestfallen.

Dia put a hand on my shoulder. "That's not all. Plays and puppet shows based on this book are being performed all around the city."

"The church is scary when it gets serious, my lord," Tarte commented.

"Y-you've got that right."

I'd explained how the leaders of the Alamite Church were merchants at heart, but I had no idea how far it went. This was an absurd amount of effort. Clearly, playing politics wasn't the church's only job; propagating the faith was just as important. It was natural that the cardinals would know better than anyone how to disseminate information throughout society.

Well played, Church.

"This is great, Lugh. You're a living legend now," Dia said.

"I feel so proud," Tarte added.

"...You do understand what this means for my main profession, right?"

Pilgrims from all over would buy this book and return to their homes with multiple copies as souvenirs. I didn't particularly mind the name Lugh Tuatha Dé becoming widely recognized, but having your face printed on the cover of a book was fatal for an assassin.

Dia laughed. "Ah-ha-ha, whoops. You've become the most famous person in the world."

"You can always disguise yourself while on the job!" Tarte offered.

Perhaps it was best to look at this positively. There were surely numerous ways to take advantage of this sudden fame.

"Anyway, let's get dinner. At a restaurant with private rooms, preferably," I suggested.

"Yeah, it'd be difficult to eat with everyone ogling us," Dia agreed.

Tarte gasped. "Oh-oh, I messed up."

"What do you mean, Tarte?"

"You said you wanted to eat out, my lord, so I searched for good restaurants... And the one I picked doesn't have private rooms."

She looked dejected. I didn't ask Tarte to find a place for us. She'd taken the initiative as a favor, so I understood why she felt so down about the mistake.

"You made a mistake, but your heart was in the right place. Next time, think a little harder about our needs when you make a decision," I ordered.

"Yes, my lord. I'll do better next time!" Tarte exclaimed.

I patted her on the head and started walking. I'd investigated every corner of this city and knew plenty of good restaurants with private rooms, but I elected not to say anything. Tarte put real effort into finding a dinner spot. Entrusting this to her would help her grow, and it sounded like good fun.

The holy city had a great variety of shops, a by-product of the diverse travelers who visited. People of all races, cultures, and customs walked the streets, and the full financial spectrum was on display as well. There were plenty of rich customers, but there were restaurants serving the less wealthy, too. Our chosen restaurant was a slightly pricey option for middle-class patrons.

"Hey, this place is nice," I said.

Tarte looked pleased. "I am glad you like it."

"Lugh's always been a fan of this sort of establishment," Dia remarked.

"I like good food in a more laid-back atmosphere."

High-class restaurants with strict dress codes and etiquette made it difficult to relax. However, if a restaurant was too inexpensive, the dishes would suffer from cheap ingredients and poorly compensated employees to keep costs down. Restaurants of this grade used fair ingredients and allowed their employees the time necessary to serve quality food, but it didn't require the clientele to act formally.

It was my favorite way to dine. Tarte knew my tastes well.

"I like this kind of restaurant, too. Expensive restaurants are too stiff and boring," Tarte agreed.

"Tarte. I get what you're saying, and I'm sure you chose this place because of Lugh's preferences. But Lugh is a noble, and you're his personal retainer. Both of you need to get used to high-class establishments. You'll be visiting more of them in the future, whether you like it or not." Dia was in full-on big sister mode.

House Viekone, Dia's family, was composed of major nobles from Soigel. Dia was raised to maintain perfect table manners. Even the way she used her silverware was beautiful.

"You have a point. We can't be too picky. I'm beyond exhausted, though. At times like this, I just want to enjoy myself," I responded.

"Yeah, I'll give you a pass today. But next time, you should pick the most expensive and stuffy restaurant you can find. You both need training."

"You just want to eat at a high-class place."

"No, not particularly. I've had enough of that kind of food. I like your home cooking the most."

Dia's favorite food was my gratin, a surprising pick for one of her standing. Gratin was thought of as restaurant food in Japan, but it was a classic home dish. The ingredients were cheap, and it was easy to make. It had a folksy appeal.

"Got it. We'll go to an expensive place next time. Don't hold back on my training," I said.

"Heh-heh, what are big sisters for? I'll turn you into a pro," Dia answered.

The first wave of food arrived just as Dia's surge of big sister behavior settled. I went with the chef's choice—that was the most fun thing to do when visiting a restaurant for the first time.

"This salad isn't very fresh," Dia complained.

"Yeah, it's mushy," Tarte agreed.

"There's nothing they can do about that. The holy city doesn't grow vegetables, and imported ones lose freshness during transport," I explained.

"But the royal capital and Milteu had fresh greens."

"That's not the norm for large cities. The capital and Milteu are trying to improve their food self-sufficiency in preparation for potential sieges."

Being able to eat fresh vegetables was a luxury. It was possible in the royal capital and Milteu because they were large cities with plans for demon and monster attacks or invasions by foreign nations. The capital and Milteu had fields to grow crops inside the city walls.

It was nonsensical from a business perspective to grow crops on such expensive land. Many believed the cities should get rid of the fields to make room for shops and homes, and buy vegetables from elsewhere. I opposed that mindset, however. I believed that large cities should secure food without relying on external help.

"Wow, I didn't realize how much thought went into stuff like that," Dia said.

"I'm sure the Viekone domain was self-sufficient, too," I replied.

"Yeah, it was. The Viekone domain was large, wealthy, and rich with tradition, but we were far from the capital, and our trade wasn't very developed. We actually exported leftover food, now that I think about it."

"Really?"

"Yep. Viekone produced the most food in Soigel. Our wheat fields stretched as far as the eye could see in autumn. It was beautiful... We'll have to visit Viekone when it's restored. I'll show you around."

"Yeah, definitely."

"It's a promise."

House Viekone fell to ruin after siding with the royal faction and losing during Soigel's civil war. Dia's father was hiding, building strength to hopefully restore his domain one day.

"I might be able to lead an army and recover the Viekone domain, now that I'm a saint," I remarked.

My new title carried a lot of power. I could change public opinion in an instant by claiming that the Soigelian royal family was just. The noble faction only won the civil war because of Setanta Macness's abnormal strength, and he was no longer around. I could reclaim Viekone for Dia with some effort.

"I'd be furious if you did that. I want my domain back, but I'd worry over the repercussions of relying on corrupt external aid... Dad said he'll restore our home, and I know he'll succeed. All I can do now is wait for him to ask for help. That, and better myself so I can meet his expectations."

"You're really strong, Dia."

"I'm a Viekone, after all. Will you support us when the time comes?"

There was no reason for an assassin of the Alvanian Kingdom to help a Soigelian noble. However...

"What husband could refuse aiding his wife's family?"

"D-don't just spring words like 'husband' and 'wife' on me. That's embarrassing."

"What do you mean? We're engaged."

"That's true, but... Geez, little brothers aren't supposed to be so cheeky."

Dia sipped her soup to hide her embarrassment. I couldn't help but chuckle—she managed to look beautiful even with gestures like that.

"I'm not impressed by the salad and soup, but maybe the entrée will be better. If it disappoints, I'm blaming Tarte for choosing this place," Dia stated, forcibly changing the conversation.

"Huh? I–I'm sure it will be delicious!" Tarte insisted, flustered.

"Relax. See how many customers there are? A bad restaurant wouldn't pack the seats," I assured her.

The food arrived as if in answer—roast lamb seasoned with rock salt. It smelled wonderful, likely because it was wrapped in herbs while being cooked. This technique prevented meat from drying out and enhanced its aroma. I often used it myself.

We followed the waiter's instructions and picked up the meat by the bones to eat.

"Wow, this is amazing," Dia praised.

"It really is. Such a rich flavor," Tarte agreed.

I nodded. "…This meat was aged."

Meat didn't necessarily taste its best when fresh. Protein required time to gain flavor. Thus, allowing meat to sit before cooking it was typical. This restaurant took it further by aging the meat. This went beyond letting it sit. Employees adjusted the humidity and ventilation of the storage room to create the desired environment. That was the only way to achieve this taste.

"This more than makes up for that salad," Dia said.

"I agree. It's so good I want a second helping," Tarte declared.

"…I wonder if the restaurant or the butcher is responsible for aging the meat. If it's the latter, I'll have to buy some for myself," I mumbled.

Dia frowned. "Lugh, no talking about work while we're eating!"

A few more dishes followed the entrée. Mutton was the primary local meat. The holy city was landlocked, which meant no

fishing. Nearby villages that raised livestock came to favor lamb over time because the cold climate of this region created a high demand for wool.

"The meat dishes were all really good," I said.

"Yeah, I'm more than satisfied," Dia agreed.

"Was that the last course?" Tarte asked.

"No, there's still dessert... Here it comes."

Our final dish was cheesecake with sheep cheese.

"Ugh, this stinks," Dia complained.

"You really think so? I don't mind," Tarte said.

Sheep's milk had a peculiar scent that intensified when made into cheese. Many struggled to eat it, even in Europe, where people consumed ten times more cheese than in Japan. I didn't like it much, either, but I pushed myself to give it a try.

"...The smell is a hurdle, but it's good. It has a stronger flavor than cow cheese."

Tarte bobbed her head. "I like it a lot."

Following our example, Dia reluctantly used her fork to cut herself a small piece of cake and eat it. "...It's not terrible, but *man*, I don't think I can handle any more. That stench is inescapable." She washed down the rest of the cheese in her mouth with alcohol.

"I am so sorry. I should have performed a more careful investigation. I know Lord Lugh would have been able to find a restaurant you would like, Lady Dia," Tarte apologized.

"Oh, don't get me wrong, Tarte. This was a great meal. I didn't love the salad or dessert, but the meat was delicious. I'm satisfied," Dia said.

"Um, so you really liked this place?"

"Totally. I want you to keep taking me to new restaurants.

I'll never encounter new tastes if you only choose restaurants that serve my favorites. I don't like this dessert, but it was a fun new experience."

That way of thinking was very like Dia. She was a curious and adventurous soul, my total opposite. That was probably what attracted me to her.

Dia put a finger to her lips. "You know, I don't think I've ever seen you be picky about food, Tarte. Do you like everything? You're not just pretending to like it for Lugh's sake, are you?"

Tarte tilted her head as she chewed on a bite of cheesecake. "No, I have never thought that way about food. I was always hungry before Lord Lugh found me, and I'd eat anything I could, regardless of taste. I truly mean it when I say 'anything.' Rotten food was far from the worst of what I ate... I often consumed things only used for ingredients. I've never thought anything was too gross to eat."

Dia looked awkward. She'd lived an impossibly luxurious life in comparison to Tarte, who spent her early years starving.

"I, uh... I'm sorry, Tarte. That was insensitive of me."

"Don't worry about it. We were just raised with different values. Also, House Viekone took good care of its hardworking citizens, right?"

"Yeah, we did. I'm proud that no one died for lack of food in Viekone after Dad took over. He took measures to prevent that from happening, like storing food to distribute whenever there was a bad harvest."

I'd researched the Viekone domain a lot in preparation to help Dia reclaim the region someday. I'd feigned ignorance for the sake of conversation when we were talking about vegetables earlier.

"That is wonderful... There is nothing I hate more than evil nobles who exploit their people to the point of starvation so they can live in luxury," Tarte said.

Tarte's home domain bordered Tuatha Dé. It was blessed with good weather and soil, and the people would have been able to live in comfort if not for the awful ruler. He took everything from his citizens and wasted money on his own luxury. When the citizens' productivity worsened because of their suffering, he responded by raising taxes. That further lowered the quality of life and productivity, creating a hellish place to live.

People had no choice but to sell themselves into slavery or abandon their elderly and children. Tarte was one of those cast out. It's why she hated nobles who lived in excess, especially those who mistreated their subjects.

"Hey, what would you have done if House Viekone was a wicked noble family?" Dia asked.

"Nothing. I'd keep my hatred for you to myself," Tarte responded.

Dia's face stiffened. It was almost better to have someone hate you openly than to hold a silent grudge.

"Good thing you managed your domain well," I said.

Dia sighed. "You've got that right. I need to thank Dad and my ancestors."

Tarte ate the rest of the cake unbothered by the awkward atmosphere. She looked happy as could be. Dia and I were both taken aback.

I truly was glad I found Tarte in the mountains that winter. I wouldn't have been able to save her otherwise, nor would I have obtained such a lovely and diligent servant.

The festival was only three days away, and the city was rife with excitement. All who were here to do business had determined looks in their eyes, whether they were part of a large company or selling products as individuals. The bigger the festival, the more money to be made. This was no ordinary celebration, either. It was being held in the holy city, and the Alamite Church had reached out to all countries for cooperation. This was a perfect opportunity to gain fame.

I was taking a stroll through the city on my own. Nobody addressed me. That wasn't because the Lugh Tuatha Dé boom was over. On the contrary, the craze had worsened—the book was flying off the shelves, and plays and puppet shows were gaining popularity.

I moved unnoticed because I was disguised. *No one has any idea who I am. Looks like my fame is going to have no impact on my assassin trade.* I concealed my identity both to avoid being swarmed and to see if people would recognize me. This was the epicenter of my sudden popularity. If no one here saw through my facade, I'd have no trouble continuing my assassination work.

I wasn't thrilled with the option, but I could alter my face with plastic surgery if my disguise wasn't sufficient. Changing the contour of my face, the length of my nose, or the shape of my eyes would make me look like a completely different person. I would have done that without hesitation in my past life. I'd changed my face multiple times, in fact.

I didn't want to do that anymore, however. I didn't want to betray the love of my three fiancées.

"What are you doing, Lugh Tuatha Dé?"

I gasped. The voice sounded like a man's, but it was a little high. Did someone see through my disguise? I hid my agitation and kept walking, ignoring the voice like an unrelated person would.

"I'm talkin' to you, buster. You really think that disguise is gonna work?"

The person addressed me again. Their voice was a little higher this time; they were straining their voice to change it. It was likely they were a woman. I didn't know why they were pretending to be a man... *Wait. I know what's going on here.*

This was a prank, and I knew the culprit.

"Stop joking around, Maha. You almost gave me a heart attack."

I turned around to see a beautiful girl who appeared wise beyond her years. She was wearing light makeup, and her clothes were modest but fashionable. The male voice I'd heard earlier came from her. Maha had no talent for combat, but I'd trained her in various other fields. She knew how to change her voice.

"Drat, you found me out." Maha smiled with a ladylike grace that could not have been more at odds with the gruff male voice she'd produced.

"You've still got a ways to go," I responded.

"I've been too busy to practice. I admit defeat... Anyway, welcome home, dear brother."

"It's good to be back, Maha."

This obviously wasn't my home, but I could tell Maha wanted to have that exchange, so I obliged.

The Alamite Church called on businesses from all over the world, so naturally, it reached out to Natural You, the cosmetics brand rapidly gaining popularity all over.

Maha and I were in the store Natural You was using during the festival. Lower-ranking companies had to share the floor of a building with other enterprises, but we were given an entire store with a good location. We'd have to meet some high expectations.

"Good afternoon, Mr. Illig and Ms. Maha."

Everyone we passed greeted us with hasty bows. I was currently disguised as Illig Balor, the illegitimate, prostitute-born child of the Balor Company's president. I founded Natural You under this identity with support from the Balor Company. That was why everyone addressed me so formally.

Maha and I entered an office and locked the door.

"I'm impressed you made it. It usually takes longer than a week to travel here from Milteu," I said.

Horse-drawn carriages were much slower than one might think. A horse couldn't run for half a day without getting tired, and they could only manage about twelve kilometers per hour, slower than a bike. No matter how much you hurried, it took at least a week to make the trip from Milteu.

"You have no idea the effort it took. Instead of a carriage I raced here on horseback, trading for the fastest horse I could find at every village I passed. Whenever I couldn't get a horse,

I strengthened myself with mana and ran instead… It would've been a lot easier if you made good on your promise to give me a hang glider," Maha replied.

"Sorry. I haven't been able to find the time."

In an era where even the main roads weren't well maintained, being able to ignore topography and move at high speeds in the air was incredibly useful. That's why I wanted to make a hang glider for Maha, but I kept having to put it off because of all the recent trouble. Maha's elemental affinity being water was also an issue. Figuring out how to power the hang glider would be difficult.

"Don't worry, I know everything you've been through… I have to apologize as well. Duke Romalung approached me personally and pressed me into admitting what I do for you and the existence of the telecommunications network."

"There was nothing you could do once he found you. Not even I can hide all my secrets from that monster. I'm at fault for underestimating him."

"Had I known there was such a formidable person out there, I would've taken the proper measures to ensure he didn't discover me."

"Act too carefully, though, and we lose our greatest weapon—the speed at which we gather information."

Certain restrictions were necessary to prevent an information network's secrets from being discovered. It was a trade-off between safety and results. The information network wouldn't turn up much if we played it overly safe because of Duke Romalung.

"Yeah, that's a difficult balance."

"For now, he's an ally. Just make sure you're not discovered by anyone else. Let's maintain the status quo."

"You got it. I admit I also gave him documents because he said he needed them to save you."

"I was at the meeting when he used them. They did end up saving me. You made the right call."

"I'm glad to hear that."

I doubted that Maha gave Duke Romalung the documents simply because of a threat. As my information network's manager, Maha saw all information collected. That enabled her to confirm my situation and decide that sharing the data with the duke was the best decision. I left her in charge because she could make calls like that.

Maha was the best person I knew at information analysis and decision-making. She wasn't fit for combat, but honestly, her talents were much rarer. She was irreplaceable.

"I don't know what I would've done without you," I said.

Intel was your sword and shield against political schemes. I had no choice but to work Maha to the bone on such occasions. Overseeing Natural You was a significant burden on its own, but Maha was the only person I could trust to handle my company and information network.

"No need to thank me. I was doing my job, and I'm happy to be of help to you... But I will accept an apology if you insist," Maha responded.

I smiled. She always tried to play it cool when asking for things from me.

"I do insist. What can I do to make up for this?"

"Hug me tight and kiss me. I've been so lonely without you."

I embraced Maha's thin body and kissed her. She put her tongue in my mouth. Clearly, she'd been studying hard.

We moved apart after we finished kissing.

"I forgive you." Maha tried to appear mature and calm, but her flushed cheeks and the tremor in her voice gave away her embarrassment. I found that side of her adorable.

"Is that really all you need? It's not like you to let me off the hook so easily."

"...Hee-hee, you're right. Stay by my side a little longer."

Surprise showed on Maha's face for a moment, but she quickly resumed her relaxed act and took my outstretched hand with ladylike grace. She hesitated and blushed slightly when our hands touched. Maha didn't have it in her to be a bad girl.

"I'll stay with you as long as you like, my princess."

"I'm no princess... But thank you."

A spring entered Maha's step. She was in a great mood. Evidently, I'd see plenty of her cute side today. I wanted to spoil her as much as I could, and not simply because I frequently worked her so hard.

My date with Maha was underway. We were taking a break in a café after spending some time visiting famous tourist spots. It wasn't long before we ended up discussing work. Dia hated talking about real life during our dates, but Maha was the opposite—she continually brought it up. She likely thought of business as a hobby rather than just a job.

"You said you rushed here using the fastest horses you could find, but how did you get the staff and product needed for the festival?" I asked.

I'd been wondering about that all day. Maha could accomplish difficult feats on her own using her power as a mage, but how did she get everything else here in time? She didn't have any special items like my Leather Crane Bag to make transporting easier. Setting up a temporary Natural You store in the holy city by herself was nearly impossible.

"I got lucky. I'm in the process of opening a Natural You branch in a nearby town. I sent orders to that branch via carrier pigeon when I left Milteu, requesting to borrow the staff and stock for the celebration. I planned on holding a grand opening sale, so the branch had plenty of stock," Maha explained.

"Oh yeah, you put that in your report."

Natural You currently consisted of its headquarters in Milteu, one branch in the royal capital, and another in Maha's hometown. I'd heard that she wanted to open another branch, but I didn't know it was near the holy city.

"A flood of pilgrims visits the holy city every day. I'm opening the branch to capitalize on those customers. I wanted a store in the holy city, but I had to settle for a town twenty kilometers away."

"I'm sure it's hard to establish a business here, even for a company of our stature."

There were a great many enterprises competing for a coveted spot in the holy city. Many of them wanted in for religious purposes, not just for profit. The waitlist was years long, and even opening a small shop cost a fortune. To make matters more difficult, money wasn't enough—you needed powerful connections as well.

"Yeah, that might be a pipe dream. Even the price of land in the nearby town was insane... The lord of the domain helped us out because he happens to be a Natural You fan, but it's going to take a while for us to get a return on our investment."

The profit margin of Natural You's cosmetics, the business's main focus, was extremely high. That applied to all cosmetics. In my past world, it was common for skin lotion to sell for one hundred times what it cost to make. We weren't that egregious—most of our products sold for about ten times the production expense. The price of opening the branch must have been enormous if earning back the investment would take a while.

"Even if the branch loses us money, the price will be more than worth it if we consider it an advertising expense. We'll gain a lot by serving customers in the holy city," I said.

Maha nodded. "Exactly. That's why I decided to go ahead with it."

Pilgrims came from all over the world to visit the holy city. Selling to them would spread our products far and wide. The new branch might not make a profit, but the cost would be cheap, considering the publicity it would bring. It was an example of Maha's incredible wit as a merchant that she was able to make that call.

"If you've got staff and our regular product covered, then we have to think up a special item suitable for the festival," I said.

"I was worried about that. I'm sure we'd make a fortune just selling our regular merchandise, but that's not enough to leave a mark on the celebration, I suppose," Maha replied.

"Natural You is still a young company. You could consider our lack of experience with this kind of event a weakness of ours. We were given a great location—we have a duty to live up to the expectation."

Festivals were special occasions, and companies tried to rise to the occasion by offering unique goods that couldn't be bought anywhere else.

"I understand that, but I think it's a little ridiculous they expect us to prepare in a week."

Companies normally spent half a year preparing for something like this. Product development was a lengthy process.

"These difficult circumstances are the perfect opportunity to set ourselves apart from the pack... We were finally able to improve our production lines, too. I want to use this chance to reach more people."

Natural You had never been able to keep up with demand. Our production lines were less than adequate, and our inability to serve all our customers meant there was no point in trying to increase popularity. I had viewed this as an issue since the first store opened, and we'd only recently succeeded at increasing production.

Keeping the recipe for Natural You's flagship product, moisturizer, a secret was what made increased production challenging. If the formula got out, anyone could easily fabricate an imitation. Rival companies regularly attempted to bribe our employees or sent secret agents into our factories, so we had to stay on guard.

"I want to impress, but I'm at a dead end. Which means it's your turn, dear brother," Maha said.

"What, are you leaving this product entirely to me?" I asked.

Maha wore a teasing expression. "Says the guy who counts on me to run Natural You by myself year-round. You need to step up and do some work every now and then, too. Let's go back to the store."

Work on a product didn't end with its development. You also had to produce a sufficient supply, package everything, and explain the item to employees. That left us only one day to work on development.

"No, let's continue our date for a little longer," I responded.

"You're not giving up, are you? We won't get anywhere by hiding from reality."

"No matter what we make, we'll need materials, right? Given our limited time, the product has to be something we can manufacture in good quantity while remaining within budget against the resources available in the city. It would be most efficient for us to continue our date and look at shops to figure out what we can make."

"Ah, that's a good plan."

"Also..." I trailed off, too embarrassed to continue.

"Go on."

"You work so hard for me. I want to show my appreciation. Is a date sufficient?"

Maha giggled and gave me her best smile. "Yes, and then some. Let's head out."

She stood and urged me to do the same. After taking my hand, she leaned against me as we left the café.

We walked to a shopping district. The variety of businesses in the holy city truly was astounding. There were plenty of souvenir stores offering goods that came very close to breaking the rule against selling items related to the church.

"That book has to be exceeding every sales record," Maha said.

"Please, don't bring it up. I get a headache just looking at that fairy tale drawing of myself," I grumbled.

"The book was actually pretty interesting... I want to hire the author. They couldn't have had more than one or two days to draft it."

"Yeah."

That book was written absurdly fast. It was put to print three days after I killed the Puppeteer demon, which gave the author only two days to create the story. They likely had to deal with a long list of meticulous requests as well, including giving each of the cardinals a moment to shine and fitting the signature line into the last scene. That was to say nothing of the most important mission of improving the image of the Alamite Church. Only a talented author could have completed this book on such a short deadline while satisfying all their clients' demands.

"The author's name isn't in the book," Maha noted.

"It was probably left out in the interest of disseminating the church's 'truth.' They decided it would be best for people to not think about the author of the story," I explained.

"That makes sense… Excuse me, can I please buy five copies of that novel? Oh, really? It's only three per person…? Then I'd like three of them delivered to the building where Natural You…"

"Hey."

Maha ignored me and finished checking out.

"What are you playing at?" I asked.

"Oh, come on. You— *Ahem*, Lugh Tuatha Dé is so cool in this book. I have to buy it. I've already purchased a personal copy, but I want more as souvenirs. I think Mother will love it."

An image of Mom gushing over how cool her "little Lugh" was while hugging me flashed through my mind.

"…I'm sure she would, but I wouldn't be able to take it. Please don't do this to me."

"Hee-hee, no promises."

"What are the other two for?"

"One is a spare and the other is for Tarte. She won't buy a copy in front of you, but I'm sure she wants one very badly."

"How kind of you."

"She's a friend… Actually, I'm not sure I think of her as a friend anymore."

"Tarte would cry if she heard that."

Maha was Tarte's best friend.

"No, that's not what I mean. 'Friend' just doesn't feel right… She's more of a clumsy and cute little sister. Yeah, that's it. That might be why I don't get too jealous of all the time she spends with you." Maha clapped her hands and nodded as though satisfied.

"So she's family."

"Once your harem is complete, we'll have to make our family official on the register."

"I don't know how I feel about the word *harem*."

"What else would you call it?"

Ouch. In noble society, people would call Dia my first wife and Tarte and Maha my concubines, but I wasn't comfortable with that, either.

"We're a team."

Maha giggled. "We're certainly more than that."

We continued to look around the shopping district as we talked. When we entered the back alleys, we found fewer shops geared at tourists and more that primarily served other businesses. Nothing gave me the inspiration I was looking for, though.

"Any good ideas yet, Illig?" Maha asked.

"I have a few, but I can do better. Let's look around a little more." There were a couple of candidates. I could throw something together using the city's resources, but I wanted a quality product.

"I've always liked your refusal to settle."

"You're the only one who would put up with this."

We kept walking until we reached the end of the shopping district. There was a church at the end of the street. Unlike the cathedral, which was built to flaunt the authority of the Alamite Church, this was a more compact establishment that also served as an orphanage.

There were children in the yard selling candles made of beeswax. It didn't look like their business was going particularly well. Cheap oil lamps were widespread, decreasing demand for beeswax.

"Beeswax… That could work," I muttered.

These orphanages received little from the church's headquarters to give the kids comfortable lives, necessitating side businesses to make more money. Beekeeping was the primary industry in this quarter of the city. It was time-consuming and came with the risk of getting stung, but it didn't require much strength, making it accessible to children. This region's climate was too cold to grow sugarcane, driving up the price of sugar and creating a high demand for honey as a sweetener. Beekeepers earned a decent amount. They could also sell beeswax.

"What are you staring at that church's yard for?" Maha asked.

"Maha. If you had to divide cosmetics into two major categories, how would you do it?" I questioned.

"Hmm… Broadly speaking, I'd divide it into skin care and makeup. The first is for improving the condition of skin, like Natural You's signature moisturizer. The latter is for enhancing one's appearance. Lipstick falls into that category."

"If we were to make a new Natural You product, what should it be for?"

"Skin care," Maha answered immediately.

"Why? Skin care is our core business, but we could find a new market if we put effort into a makeup line," I argued.

"I disagree. The makeup market is too competitive and difficult to break into. It's better to play to our strengths than to take on that challenge. Natural You became successful by making novel skin care products. We are associated with bringing out women's original beauty, not embellishing it, and we should protect that image."

I nearly grinned at the perfect answer. I'd taught my pupil well.

"That's right. It's important that we use festivals like this one to convey what makes Natural You special."

I approached the kids in the yard and told them I'd buy their entire stock of beeswax, including what they had in reserve. They excitedly sprinted into the church and returned with handfuls of containers.

"What are you going to do with all these candles, Illig? I thought you wanted to make a cosmetic product," Maha said.

"Yeah, I am. I'm buying them for the beeswax. I can use it to make something great."

Beeswax was formed from honeycombs, making it safe to digest. It was perfect for the item that would convey Natural You's core message.

"I can't imagine how a candle can be used for cosmetics."

"I think you'll like it once you see the finished product. Also, I'm not just using this beeswax because it's a good ingredient. It will add value that will make this new commodity into the perfect festival item… I need to speak with the priest."

Quality wasn't the only factor that determined a product's success—the packaging and added value mattered, too. I had to negotiate with the priest to ensure I could present this product how I envisioned.

Chapter 6 | The Assassin Makes Cosmetics

I got to work after we returned to the temporary Natural You store. I was using a kitchen installed in the office, which meant no professional equipment found in a workshop. Fortunately, this cosmetic could be made in any kitchen.

Employees from the branch watched me at a distance. My excellent hearing meant I picked up all their whispering; it was clear they admired Illig Balor and thought of him as a legend for founding Natural You.

"Will you really be able to make anything with so few tools, Illig?" Maha inquired.

"Absolutely. This product isn't difficult to create," I responded.

I laid out the ingredients on the counter. There were only three.

The first was grape seed oil, derived from grape seeds removed in the process of making white wine. Natural You sold it as a product. The oil was soft and fragrant, unsurprising, given its origin. It was expensive because of the time and effort necessary to produce it, but it remained popular.

The next was an essential oil extracted from a plant. This volatile substance was part of many Natural You products. I found the herb it came from by the sea after a prolonged search for the ideal aroma. The oil raised the quality of the company's goods, and its fragrance had become associated with the brand.

The beeswax I bought from the church was the final ingredient. It was collected from honeycombs, which bees constructed using their naturally secreted wax.

"Are those all the ingredients?" Maha inquired.

"Yes. This is a simple product, but it's high quality and original. I'm using the grape seed oil and essential oil because they're key Natural You ingredients. This beeswax is of only average quality, but being produced at a local church gives it special meaning," I explained.

"Oh, I see what you mean. I can't imagine anything better for the celebration."

Maha figured out why I was using the beeswax from that explanation alone. She really was smart.

I poured grape seed oil and beeswax into a pot and placed it in hot water to warm. Once the beeswax melted, I mixed the ingredients together and added the essential oil. All that remained was to pour it into a lipstick container and wait for it to cool. Typically, I'd let it sit for half a day, but I used magic to remove the heat and harden it because I wanted to demonstrate this new creation immediately.

"It's done," I announced.

"What is it? It's shaped like lipstick," Maha asked.

"It's called lip balm. You could call it moisturizer for your lips, I suppose. Natural You has released an array of products for skin protection, but none for the lips. We live in a dry climate, so there's more than enough need… I noticed your lips were a little chapped when we kissed earlier, and I decided I would make this when I saw the beeswax," I said.

Maha touched her lips, embarrassed. *She has nothing to be ashamed of.* Lips were delicate. Wind in dry climates damaged them over time, and a stressful job like Maha's only worsened the deterioration. I made this lip balm for people like her, who struggled with chapped lips.

"Geez, you can be so insensitive... Also, you have to be careful," Maha whispered.

She was worried because I recently got engaged to her as Lugh Tuatha Dé, and I was in disguise as Illig Balor. Maha and Illig had always been close, to the point that people suspected they were dating. The sight of Maha flirting with Illig despite being betrothed to Lugh could start some problematic rumors.

"You're worrying too much... Anyway, I'd rather fix your lips than fret about being insensitive and pretend not to notice. Let me apply this, Maha."

I placed my hand on Maha's chin to turn her face toward mine and applied my new lip balm. The employees all started talking at the sight. Maha then touched her lips.

"They're so smooth. And they don't hurt at all."

"This item is for protecting your lips. It can be used on rough hands as well... It's a medicine as well as a cosmetic," I said.

"Is it really okay to apply candle wax to your lips?"

"Beeswax comes from honeycomb, which is edible. It's completely safe."

That's why I used beeswax to make this lip balm. The ingredients had to be safe because they went on the mouth. Beeswax also had the advantage of a high melting point, which meant it wouldn't melt from body temperature or hot weather. The oils I added to make the beeswax smooth and easy to apply were sourced from grape seeds and herbs. You could even eat the lip balm if you wanted.

"I like it. Not being able to apply lipstick would kill it for me, though… Lipstick is a necessity at official events," Maha said.

"You can apply lipstick over the balm. It protects your mouth from lipstick, too," I informed her.

"Really? That's a lifesaver. Putting lipstick over dry lips is painful and makes them take longer to heal."

This creation would sell because it fit Natural You's skin care specialty.

"The only problem is that rival companies will be quick to produce imitations, unlike with moisturizer," I said.

Moisturizer was impossible to make without a special ingredient extracted from soybeans that allowed water and oil to mix. As long as that element remained a secret, no one else could imitate the moisturizer. Anyone who studied the lip balm would figure out how to make it immediately. All they needed to know was that it used oil to protect the lips—there were many ways to create it.

"That's nothing to worry about. I said earlier that it would be difficult to catch up in the makeup market because the other brands are too strong, but the reverse is true for skin care. That's our domain, and we'll easily squash those who try to copy us." Maha didn't fall for my little test. She'd long overtaken me as a businessperson. "There's something else you haven't talked about yet, dear Illig."

"What's that?"

"The reason you used beeswax."

"Oh, yeah. Tell me why you think I used it."

Maha eyed me seriously, like a student taking an exam. "Selling something that was made with resources bought from the church will give us an unbeatable advantage in a city full of pilgrims from across the world. People who buy souvenirs here want to take home a piece of the Alamite Church's power. What could be better than an item directly connected to the church? There's little demand for the beeswax on its own, but giving it a practical use by putting it into a cosmetic will lead to explosive sales."

"That's correct. I have nothing left to add."

"That's why you negotiated with the priest. You were checking if it was okay to sell beeswax made by a church."

That negotiation was the most important step. The Alamite Church would have retaliated violently if I used its name without permission.

"Exactly. The priest turned out to be a good man, and he allowed me to use the beeswax on the condition of a small donation from our sales. That enables us to sell this lip balm as a cosmetic that carries the blessing of the Alamite Church. Believers will eat them up, and they'll make good souvenirs, too."

"It's the perfect feature product for this event... It's clear that I haven't caught up to you yet, Illig. You thought up this viciously good idea and made it into a product after one day of walking around the city."

Maha looked conflicted. She was proud of me but disappointed to discover she hadn't surpassed me in business.

"You're overestimating the difficulty of what I did. Product development is nothing more than a puzzle to solve by piecing together your experiences. You need wit and intuition, but that's not what I'm asking of you. You have the talent to protect this company and grow it. That's what's expected of company executives like you."

The chief executive didn't have to work on product development. They just had to hire people with the skill. However, a chief executive was the only one capable of steering the ship.

"I know, but I'm still upset. All right, I have a declaration. Within a year, I'm going to make a hit product without your help."

"Competitive as ever, I see."

"What merchant isn't?"

Maha really was a strong and intelligent girl. I could rest easy knowing Natural You was in her hands.

"I look forward to your new item. But first, we need to prepare for the festival. You've given the lip balm your approval, so let's make it our feature product. We need to mass-produce it and nail down the packaging. Time is short."

"You're right. This is a race against time. We're counting on you all." Maha faced the employees, who replied energetically and gathered around us.

I could tell they were good workers. Maha must have put a lot of effort into finding them. I had total confidence in this product, and I couldn't have asked for a better staff. Undoubtedly, this festival would be a success.

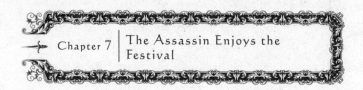

The celebration was to be held over three days, and the canonization ceremony was tomorrow evening.

The actual ritual was scheduled on the second day for a reason. If the church held the main event on the first day, the number of guests would dramatically decrease over the following two. If they held it on the third day, the first wouldn't be exciting. That made the evening of the second day the perfect choice. Many guests would want to arrive a day early, and because the ceremony was in the evening, plenty would decide to stay the night and enjoy the day after, too.

I could learn from the church's business acumen.

"We can have all the fun we want today... Uh, what should we call you?"

We were enjoying the revelry as guests. Dia was unsure of how to address me because I was in disguise. Illig was famous in his own right, so today's facade was another identity entirely. Illig was especially inconvenient with all the company executives around.

"You can just call me Lugh. Multiple people can have the same name," I responded.

"Lugh it is, then." Dia put her arm around mine.

Tarte looked on with envy. Usually, I'd ask if she wanted to

link arms, but Dia suggested that we train her to be more asser-
tive. As Dia put it, Tarte would never grow if I remained too soft
on her. Giving her what she wanted every time she made a long-
ing expression would keep her from voicing her wants. Dia had
a point, so I pretended not to notice Tarte's gaze...and felt quite
guilty doing so.

The three of us weren't alone.

"My apologies for tagging along. I don't mean to interrupt
your date."

"If you're truly sorry, Naoise, then leave."

Two people had joined our usual group. The first was a child
of the four major dukedoms, just like Nevan. His name was Naoise, and he was an elite among the elite. He came across like an
indulged pretty boy, but I'd realized after getting to know him
that he was a passionate guy who stuck to his principles.

The other tagalong missed Naoise's playful tone and grew
flustered.

"Oh, uh, should I leave, too?"

"It was a joke, Epona. I enjoy a good walk with my classmates."

"I agree. It's been so long since I've spent time with you,
Lugh. There's so much I want to talk about."

Our final member was the hero, Epona. She was the person
the goddess told me would destroy the world after killing the
Demon King. I was reincarnated in this world to slay her. She hid
her gender and presented herself as a boy, which wasn't too difficult because of her naturally androgynous appearance.

"Um, is it okay for you to be here, my lord?" Tarte asked. She
was wondering if it was all right for me to be away from the Natural You store.

I nodded. "Yeah, it's fine. That reminds me, I have a message for you from Maha. She said, 'I had my fill, so now it's your turn.'"

"Maha is too nice... I get to be with you all the time."

I was going to be tied up tomorrow because of the ceremony, but I was free to do as I wished today. It would be best for me to be at Natural You, especially because the first day was always the most difficult, but Maha had told me to go enjoy the festival.

"She really is a good girl," I agreed, although perhaps I ought to have called her a woman, not a girl. "Oh yeah, there's something I've been meaning to ask. I know Epona has been getting sent all over the place as the hero, but what have you been up to all week, Naoise?"

Naoise was no longer just my classmate—he was also the pawn of a demon. Seeking greater power, he'd entered the service of Mina, the snake demon I'd formed an alliance with. That agreement meant I didn't have to fight him, but it didn't change the fact that he'd betrayed humanity. I needed to remain wary of him. I'd assigned spies to follow him, but he'd escaped them all.

"Being the son of a duke comes with its own fetters. There are always many people I need to greet in cities like this," he responded.

That was a lie. I would have known if that was what he was doing. Clearly, he'd been on some errand for Mina.

"Be careful, Naoise. I want us to remain friends," I said.

"I want the same. You are a very dear friend to me... That's why I'm interrupting your date to spend time with you." Naoise smiled and put a hand on my shoulder opposite the arm Dia held.

"As much as I value your friendship, Naoise, I don't need your hand on my shoulder."

"Ha-ha, that was uncomfortable for me, too... You've changed, Lugh. You've become more human."

"You make it sound like I wasn't human before."

"Exactly. You felt like... Well, *almost* human."

I froze for a moment. He was right on the mark. In my past life, I was nothing more than a puppet who followed the orders of my organization. My final wish when I was betrayed was a chance to live for myself. My life as Lugh was filled with parental love, I'd met Dia and my other friends, and I'd learned how to be a person. I thought I was already perfectly human by the time I met Naoise, but now that I thought about it, I'd still been warped.

"Don't think too hard about it. I just want to have a good time today. This may be the last chance I'll ever get to spend a fun, carefree day with you," Naoise said.

"What do you mean by that?" I questioned.

Naoise didn't answer, walking away to hit on Tarte. She grew flustered and hastily yet firmly rejected him. I was positive he did that to avoid answering my question.

I shouldn't press him on it. He likely couldn't answer. We were gathered here as classmates—for now, at least, I should forget about all the trouble we were wrapped up in.

"I've been meaning to say this, but stop trying to put the moves on Tarte," I demanded.

Naoise had been hitting on her since the day we met.

"Ah-ha-ha, I do it because I'm fond of her," Naoise responded.

Tarte bowed her head in apology.

"I'm serious. Stop. She looks miserable."

"Oh, what's the big deal? I think you just don't like people taking what you feel to be yours."

"…Yeah. That's a part of it. Tarte is my fiancée now. Leave my girl alone."

"L-Lord Lugh…," Tarte stammered, blushing deeply.

"Wow." Naoise grinned and bowed. "Please, forgive my ignorance. More has changed than I realized since we last met. I'm not shameless enough to try stealing a friend's girl."

He wore a sincere expression when he raised his head.

"…I'm not sure how to respond to that," I admitted.

"You don't have to say anything. Make Tarte happy for me. Just knowing you accept her love made this meeting worth it. That's a real comfort."

"What do you mean by that?"

"Is it strange that I wish for the girl I love to be happy?"

"No. It just feels abrupt… Wait, I thought you loved Nevan. She was quite concerned for you, as well."

I thought Nevan and Naoise had a special relationship. She always tried to help him, fretting over his well-being.

"She's more of an…older sister to me, you could say. We were both born into one of the four major dukedoms, and we've known each other since we were young. We were even engaged for a time. Duke Romalung put an end to that when he decided I didn't live up to his expectations, though. I'm apparently incapable of creating the ultimate humans… Honestly, our marriage may have been doomed to fail anyway. Nevan is a superbeing, perfect in every way. In her eyes, I'm just a worthless little brother who needs looking after. I worked so hard to prove her wrong."

That explanation made sense. Nevan's feelings for Naoise came off as more protective than romantic.

Tarte timidly raised a hand.

"Um, what made you take an interest in me, Naoise?" she asked.

"You want to know? It's because you're a cute maid with big boobs," Naoise stated.

"M-m-my boobs?" Tarte blushed and covered her chest.

"I was drawn to your personality and mannerisms as well. You're a lot like my mother. My father, who is every bit as domineering as you'd expect of a duke, had me after knocking up a maid. That gave me something of a mother complex. Actually, maybe that's not quite right... Perhaps I imagined I could upset my father by marrying a maid who resembled my mother."

Naoise laughed. He looked strange, like a weight had been lifted off his shoulders.

"Looking back on my life, I don't think I ever walked my own path. I was always concerned with proving myself to others. I wanted to get back at those in my family who thought less of me because of my lowborn blood. My father sees me as a reminder of his affair, Duke Romalung branded me unworthy and annulled the engagement, Nevan treats me as a worthless thing that needs to be looked after...and you, Lugh, decided I'm your inferior."

Deep resentment came through in Naoise's words.

"But I don't care anymore. I've found something that only I can do. Ah, this makes me feel better. I'm glad I was able to speak with you." Naoise grinned after venting his resentments, looking refreshed.

I couldn't find the words to respond. While I sank into contemplation, Dia clapped her hands to gather our attention.

"How long are you gonna ramble about yourself? Let's just enjoy the festival."

"Yeah. There are so many shops, we may not get to them all today," I said.

Tarte nodded. "It looks like there are fun activities as well."

"I agree. Let's have the best time we can today," Naoise replied.

Dia changed the mood, giving us a chance to spend time as classmates. One thing still bothered me, though. Naoise claimed he'd found something only he could do... Was it better to be glad for him and stay out of it? I couldn't shake the feeling that if I didn't stop him, he'd be corrupted beyond saving.

We spent the rest of the first day of the celebration having fun and laughing together as kids our age should. Unfortunately, I had no free time on the second day. The canonization ceremony didn't start until evening, but I had to get up early to attend one activity after another, including purifying myself in holy water, participating in a ritual to receive the goddess's blessing, and listening to a holy sermon. It was beyond tedious. Before I knew it, the sun had set, and the canonization was an hour away.

The final preparations were underway. A team of deacons fixed my hair, applied makeup, and dressed me in very formal attire. Students usually wore their uniforms for special occasions, but that wasn't going to cut it for something this big.

"This robe is supposed to be imbued with the blessing of the goddess, but I have to say I don't feel it," I remarked.

"Lugh, be careful. You can't say things like that," Dia chided. The deacons looked offended.

Dia was dressed appropriately for a saint's attendant. I didn't feel a trace of the goddess's power from her clothes, either, but the mystical beauty of her outfit gave it a strength all its own. It suited Dia's own charms frighteningly well.

"Was I the right choice for this? Looking after you is a servant's job. I hope Tarte isn't upset."

"I'll talk to her about it later," I said.

I could only take one attendant to the canonization ceremony. Dia was my immediate choice.

"You always choose me when you can only have one. I feel bad."

"I'll pick Tarte next time, then."

"Hrm, I don't think I'd be able to handle that."

I hugged Dia in reply.

"I've told Tarte and Maha that I love you the most. They both understand, and they're okay with it. It's nothing for you to worry about."

"True. I know I'm not being fair. I feel bad about you choosing me, but I still don't want to give up the privilege. If they ever take issue in the future, I'll deal with it then."

I didn't feel like that was the best plan, but I supposed it would do.

"Oh dear, must you flirt so openly? I feel like you're doing this out of spite."

Nevan and the Alam Karla entered the room. The Alam Karla was here to officiate me, and Nevan was present as her attendant.

"Think what you will," I responded.

"I'm jealous," Nevan admitted.

I ignored her teasing and discreetly gave her a covert signal. The sign was one that all Alvanian nobles learned, just as Duke Romalung had used during the meeting with the cardinals. I told her that I wanted to talk alone.

She answered in acknowledgment.

After listening to an explanation of the proceedings for the canonization ceremony, Nevan and I found a free moment to hide

behind a large church treasure and a stack of boxes. I figured we'd
be able to have a private conversation there.

Nevan grinned. "Are you inviting me on a date?"

"It's nothing so nice… I want to talk about Naoise," I said.

"Did that hopeless little brother of mine do something again?"

Little brother, huh? That truly was how Nevan thought of
Naoise.

I told her about his behavior yesterday.

"I have a bad feeling about this. He seemed strangely relaxed…
I'm worried he's going to get himself into some serious trouble.
I've assigned people to watch him, but my information network is
better at observing the larger picture than pursuing an individual."

"This is certainly concerning. All right, I will mobilize the
Romalung intelligence department. Don't expect too much,
though. We have been monitoring him since he entered that
demon's service, but he's proved elusive. He possesses some mysterious abilities that make him difficult to follow. Our elite agents
can't keep up."

If he could shake off House Romalung's elite agents, then that
didn't leave many options.

"I could follow him myself. The only others capable would
be…"

"Myself, Father, or Cian Tuatha Dé. It would require a person
of that skill."

"I doubt you or Duke Romalung have the time."

"Yes, we are both occupied with duties that will shape the
kingdom's future."

"And as for me…"

"You can forget about that. You're going to lose all your free-
dom once you become a saint."

"That leaves Dad."

"I will have the royal family send House Tuatha Dé the job. Are you sure this is what you want?"

"What do you mean?"

"You may be sending your father to his death."

Dad was going to be tailing the pawn of a demon. None of my agents had died yet, but that was only because Naoise could ditch them without attacking. Dad would keep up, forcing Naoise to get violent.

"The Tuatha Dé clan wields its blade for the Alvanian Kingdom. We are prepared to give our lives."

"Just promise you won't blame me for whatever happens."

That was the end of our conversation. I'd just saddled Dad with the dangerous task of pursuing Naoise... I was worried, but I trusted that he'd be all right. I knew that no matter what happened, he'd prioritize returning with information. He wouldn't die.

The excitement at the canonization ceremony was intense. The crowd seemed even more hectic than it did at my execution.

I emerged to joyful cheers and envious looks as I took the stage wearing the clothes supposedly blessed by the goddess. Many in the audience were taken by Dia's spellbinding beauty as she accompanied me. The experience was in stark contrast to when citizens had jeered and hurled stones at me ten days ago.

The Alam Karla waited on the stage. She held what looked like a wedding veil. *Huh, this one is the real thing.* I felt the goddess's power from the veil. It also projected power like that of a divine treasure... Perhaps that's what it was.

I knelt before the Alam Karla.

"Lugh Tuatha Dé. I, the Alam Karla, the voice of the goddess, recognize you as chosen by the divine. I bestow this veil as proof." The Alam Karla placed the object over my face. Deafening cheers erupted behind me, creating a shock wave that shook the veil. "The eighth saint in history has been born. Lugh Tuatha Dé will save us all by expelling the darkness of the demons. Everyone, join me in prayer!"

The cheering came to an immediate stop. Tens of thousands of people shut their mouths and closed their eyes. It was a bizarre sight. There was always some percentage of people in a crowd who ignored orders to be silent, but not this time.

I felt a swelling of the goddess's power. *Is this ceremony more than a simple formality?* Tens of thousands of prayers were transmitted into me and converted into strength. It was an intoxicating feeling, like I had drunk the best alcohol in the world. Then, without any signal, every person in the crowd finished, opening their eyes at once to look at me.

"Lugh Tuatha Dé, stand and speak," the Alam Karla commanded.

I stood and turned around. The words came out naturally.

"I have received your many prayers. I will make them my strength and drive away the darkness."

The crowd cheered louder than before, and passions swelled.

My eyes were drawn to one person out of the many present. It was Naoise. He gave me a carefree smile, waved, then turned and departed. It was casual behavior I'd seen from him countless times in the classroom, but it felt different this time. I didn't know why, but it gave me the feeling that I'd never see him again.

Chapter 9 | The Assassin Returns to the Academy

Naoise disappeared after the festival. Reflecting upon his behavior, I saw it was clear he intended to vanish. I should have stopped him... Although I doubt he would've listened.

My information network picked up a sign of Naoise a few days after the ceremony, and House Romalung gave the royal family an order to convey to the Tuatha Dé clan. Dad accepted the order and went after my wayward friend. *Once Dad corners Naoise, I can take action*, I thought. I couldn't do anything until then.

I returned to the academy feeling depressed. My new sainthood was the talk of the campus, and I stood out even more than I already did. I often shut myself away in my room to avoid the attention, and today was no different.

"You have a lot of letters, my lord," Tarte announced.

"Great. Don't people know we're not supposed to bring family matters to the academy?"

Students were supposed to leave behind their aristocratic ranks and obligations, but no one cut themselves off completely. It was more common for students to use our equality here as an excuse to approach others. Most of the letters were party invitations sent with the blatant intention of forming a connection with me. Some even talked directly of marriage.

"These people are shameless. We already announced our engagement." Dia puffed her cheeks out, indignant.

Word of my engagements traveled throughout aristocratic society after it was reported through official channels. The news spread like wildfire—unsurprising, given my status as a Holy Knight and demon slayer.

"We're not married yet. Aristocratic betrothals are overturned all the time. You three are also of low social status. I'm sure the high-ranking nobles feel they can stop the weddings and appease me by allowing me to keep you three as concubines," I explained.

Dia was a count's daughter, but her identity was a secret. At present, she was only the daughter of a baron. That made me a target for nobles of higher stations.

"That's so rude."

"I agree. You two need to be more careful than ever. Previously, aristocrats sent marriage proposals, aiming to strengthen their ties to the royal family. But the stakes have grown now that I'm a saint. Those same houses will be after the prestige of a direct link to the church and the goddess's blessing now. Someone might seek to eliminate my pesky fiancées."

There were plenty of precedents for that kind of thing.

"Don't worry about us, Lugh. There aren't many people out there who can defeat us," Dia said.

"That is right. You have trained us well, my lord, and given us power, too!" Tarte agreed.

Dia was a genius with magic. Tarte had no natural talent, but she was an unbelievably hard worker and had received the special Tuatha Dé education. I'd also strengthened them further using

My Loyal Knights. It was no exaggeration to say they were among the ten mightiest people in the kingdom.

"It doesn't matter how powerful you are if you're caught off guard. As an assassin, I know that better than anyone."

"Yeah, we do need to be careful. But don't forget that you've taught me how to catch people off guard as well."

"Yes, knowing how assassins operate will help us defend ourselves. The best way to stay safe would be to remain by your side at all times, my lord."

"Yeah, we should avoid acting alone whenever possible."

Sticking together was a simple plan, yet the most effective.

"Ah, a guest." Tarte hurried to the door at the sound of the bell. The visitor surprised me.

"Sorry for the intrusion. I have something I want to discuss with you, Lugh."

It was the hero, Epona. She was in casual attire and still dressed as a boy.

"I'll prepare tea and sweets," Tarte announced.

"Um, I appreciate the thought, but I want to speak with Lugh alone. It's important," Epona explained, concern visible on her face.

"Got it. Let's go outside." I felt bad about going back on my word immediately after telling Dia and Tarte that we should stick together as much as possible, but I couldn't ignore Epona.

"Thanks. This won't take long."

Epona had a sword at her hip. I watched her closely and saw that she was ready to fight... *Does she want to get rid of me?* No, that couldn't be it. She desired to battle, but there was no malice in her demeanor. Despite her strength, Epona was an amateur; she wasn't capable of hiding aggression.

Although suspicious, I followed the hero's example by equipping a sword. We left the dorm together after I checked my hidden gun and other concealed weapons.

There was a training ground built next to the dorm. It was always crowded around noon, but everyone left as soon as the sun set. Epona and I faced each other.

"I'm so sorry. There's something I've been keeping from you," she began. I waited silently for her to continue. "Naoise hasn't been human for some time now... I have a skill that allows me to sense that kind of thing. I knew something was wrong with him, but I didn't say anything."

Her eyes grew moist.

"Why did you choose to stay silent?" I asked.

"...He's not human anymore, but he's still Naoise. He's the same considerate, hardworking, and showy friend I came to know. If I'd told anyone what he's become, I would've had to kill him. I couldn't bring myself to do it." Epona clutched her sword with trembling hands. "Naoise has gotten stronger. He's still much weaker than me, but I think you and I are the only two who can stop him now."

"Huh... I know how you feel. No one wants to kill a friend. To be honest, I knew as well. He actually bragged about it to me. He said he gained a new power," I responded.

Epona's eyes went wide. "Why didn't you say anything?"

"Because I made a promise to the demon who turned Naoise into a monster."

"...So you betrayed humanity."

A hint of malice entered Epona's expression, giving me goose bumps.

"No, I didn't. I made a deal. This demon thinks of the other demons as nuisances, and she's been giving me information so I can take them out. There are demons I never would've killed without her help, and more innocents would've died. Without her information, I would've missed some battles entirely."

Epona's malice faded.

"I had no idea a demon could be cooperative."

"You've only seen the pig and the Puppeteer. There's plenty of diversity among the demons. Some flaunt their strength, and some hide out of cowardice. The Puppeteer became the hierarch because he desired to rule, and my ally enjoys human culture."

"I would've preferred not to know that."

"Will knowing they're not simple monsters make you unable to kill them?"

Epona didn't answer, but that was tacit affirmation. I waited patiently for her to continue, and she did with a determined expression.

"It makes me not want to kill them. But that doesn't mean I can't. I made a promise. I must be the sword that protects humanity."

A female knight guided Epona long ago, but she later died and became a source of agony for the hero. Curious, I looked into that woman and found some things that didn't add up. It's possible she was a reincarnated person.

Judging by my interactions with the goddess, she believed that mere strength wasn't enough to deal with the hero. Maybe she'd sent the world's greatest teacher to instruct Epona as a way of controlling the girl. Unfortunately, the attempt had failed and sent Epona into despair.

"Is that all you wanted to talk about?" I asked.

"No. I have a request." The hero drew her sword. "I've been getting weaker by the day. No one can train with me safely, and being stuck in the royal capital means I can't battle monsters and demons. I'm going to forget how to fight completely at this rate. I won't be able to protect those important to me."

I was the only person who could keep up with Epona in a fight.

"Is that really the reason for your frustration? Or do you just want to blow off some steam?"

Epona possessed a skill that made her restless during long periods without combat. It also caused her personality to change dramatically during the thrill of battle. Without that excitement as a release valve, she would grow stressed and unable to contain herself.

"Yeah, actually. I feel like I'm about to explode. Naoise kept me in check, and I don't know how long I can keep my composure without him here. So please fight me. I know you won't die."

What should I do here? Just like Epona said, Naoise protected her. He did what he could to ease her burden by deflecting and taking care of all the stressful duties the hero had to deal with. Both his position as a duke's son and his outstanding talent enabled him to do this. Not even I could have aided Epona in this way. Naoise developed an inferiority complex because of the powerful people around him, but there was plenty that only he was capable of.

Without him, Epona would have to handle the stress of her position directly. If she reached her limit, the damage would undoubtedly be immense. People I knew might get hurt. Thus, the best decision was to help the hero release some tension.

That was my excuse, anyway. Honestly, I just wanted to fight her. Epona claimed she'd weakened since the school shut down, but I'd grown stronger. I'd trained, obtained various weapons, and increased my arsenal of spells. I wanted to see how much closer I was to the hero.

"Okay. I'll fight you. We should move, though—this place is too small for you," I said.

This training ground was located in our dorm's courtyard. It was designed for humans, not the hero.

"Yeah, good thinking. Let's go to where that hill used to be. The one in the east. It's a wasteland now because of your weird spell," Epona suggested.

"That works for me."

I was bluffing. As an assassin, I preferred uneven land with lots of obstacles, but I couldn't be picky.

Epona started running, and I followed. I hoped to devise methods of saving the world without killing her, but I had to prepare for the worst. Being left with no choice but to take Epona out was never off the table. I'd do it if I had to, but only after spending every last second searching for alternatives.

There were too many things in this world I didn't want to lose. Epona was a friend, but protecting Dia and the rest of my family was more important.

How serious should I get in this fight? I needed a proper grasp of Epona's strength and what I could manage against her. However, it was important not to reveal too many of my tricks. Nothing I tried on the hero would work twice.

Standing amid the wasteland, I faced Epona alone. The view was flat in all directions, putting me at a disadvantage. We did pass through a forest to get here—that offered lots of places to hide. I could work with that.

"We don't want to kill each other here. Let's set a few rules. The match will last one minute. It will end as soon as one of us surrenders, faints, or breaks a limb. If we run out of time, it's a draw," I said.

"I like it. I wonder if you can handle my best for a full minute?" Epona responded.

Putting myself in mortal danger wasn't the only risk with fighting Epona—I could also lose My Loyal Knights. It was originally her skill, and it allowed the bearer to lend skills and a piece of their strength to a maximum of three people. The catch was that the ability could deem one of the knights unworthy if they lost a duel, rescinding the powers. That would be problematic, and it's why I suggested a time limit. The match would end in a stalemate if I survived for a minute, meaning I wouldn't lose.

A minute was a long time against an opponent of Epona's caliber. It might have been better to avoid this fight, given the risks, but getting a sense of our current gap in strength made it worth the danger.

"Naoise is a fool. He was doing plenty to contribute to world peace by keeping you in check… Yet he got it in his head that he was useless and was overwhelmed by an inferiority complex," I said.

Epona would have lost herself long ago if not for Naoise. He'd undoubtedly done an excellent service toward protecting world peace. He was also legitimately strong. Naoise felt inferior to Nevan, Epona, and me, but he compared himself to the wrong people.

Naoise was an excellent man in his own right. He overwhelmed any opponent without superhuman ability and even bettered us superhuman types in some ways. He was great at everything without specializing in any one area. I wished that he'd understood his strengths and was proud of them.

"You should have told him that. He always indirectly hinted at wanting your recognition," Epona responded.

"…I'll tell him the next time, then."

I drew my sword. The weapon was a decoy; I was best with a knife or a gun.

Then I used a spell Dia developed called Haste Bolt. It strengthened the electrical current within the body, significantly increasing reaction speed. It also bolstered physical strength. The magic was tremendously potent, but it damaged the body and threatened to render me immobile. Not even Rapid Recovery could keep up. At best, I'd last for a little over a minute. The time limit on this bout meant that wouldn't be a concern, though.

Next, I injected a drug into my neck. It also enhanced my reflexes. I could never keep up with Epona's speed, leaving me no choice but to rely on reactions to survive. This preparation should have allowed me to follow her movements.

And finally…

"Swift Wind Armor."

…I cast my favorite spell. It granted me wind-based defense that deflected attacks and allowed me to release compressed air to propel myself.

"Are you ready, Lugh?"

"Anytime. Give me your best shot, hero."

I beckoned for Epona to begin, and she smiled.

Epona charged toward me, the ground exploding at her feet. She moved silently. No, that wasn't right; she moved so fast that she outpaced the speed of sound. Thanks to my body's strengthened electrical current and the drug, I followed her, but only barely. I dodged with the minimum amount of movement possible, lacking time for anything else. She whipped past me, and a second later, an invisible hammer knocked me off my feet.

A sonic boom… Shock waves hammered the surrounding area, caused by Epona breaking the sound barrier.

She turned and charged again. I released a piece of my Swift Wind Armor to propel myself back and dodge, yet I was sent flying through the air once more. I barely managed to land safely, cracking a bone in my right arm.

I can't even touch her. But that's not a problem.

Epona was as quick as I remembered. There was enough distance between us now for me to act, though. I didn't have time to cast a spell or evade in any way besides the most optimal. However, I did have time to draw my gun and pull the trigger.

Elite gunners could ready, aim, and fire in 0.2 seconds. And that was the best I could do in my past life. Now I could strengthen myself with mana and hasten my reflexes with magic, pushing my speed to 0.1 seconds—faster than humanly possible.

This should be enough to hit her!

I shot three rounds, as one did to make sure they took down their opponent. My arms felt liable to snap despite being strengthened by mana. I'd designed the pistol's large bore for increased force and packed the bullets with as much Fahr Stone powder as possible without breaking the gun. The projectiles launched at an initial velocity of 1,020 meters per second, about three times the speed of sound and faster than an anti-materiel rifle.

I'd built the gun with the best possible suppressor, but it still wasn't enough to stop the recoil completely. This meant I had to steady the gun with my mana-strengthened arms to prevent the muzzle from wavering, and the shock wave cracked a bone in my left arm.

"Quit holding back, Lugh!"

Epona charged directly at the three bullets—each housing a force greater than an anti-tank rifle—and head-butted them out of the way.

You're joking...

Destructive energy increased the faster two objects moved toward each other. Epona charged toward those bullets faster than sound, which should have increased the force of the impact. Yet she was uninjured.

I fired the rest of the bullets in my magazine, but she deflected them all and threw a punch at my stomach once she entered point-blank range. I released my Wind Armor to propel myself backward and dampen the blow, but she was too swift. Her fist connected with my gut. There was an unpleasant crunching sound, and I was hurled away.

"Huh? That didn't feel like bone. How interesting!"

Epona tilted her head and laughed as I fell to my knees and coughed up blood. She'd broken the frame of my bulletproof vest. It was designed to break to cancel the force of an excessive blow. The vest was made of monster bones that were so light and tough they could survive the full-speed charge of a ten-ton truck, and Epona broke it with one punch. Without it, I would've lost all my ribs.

I chanted in midair to summon more Swift Wind Armor. Epona extended a hand toward me.

"Fireball."

Fireball was among the first fire spells one learned. It produced a fist-sized sphere of flame when cast by a regular mage, but the hero's version was quite different.

The burning orb turned to plasma because of its immense heat and rocketed toward me with the speed of a laser cannon. I responded by pulling a Fahr Stone engineered to produce a directional explosion from my Leather Crane Bag and throwing it. The stone exploded and scattered mithril chaff in midair, diverting the plasma away from me.

I'd managed to defend myself, but that was hardly one of Epona's best attacks. It was a beginner spell. That meant...

"Fireball."

...she was able to cast it again immediately. The new Fireball evaporated the chaff and pierced my body, distorting its shape.

Fortunately, that was just an illusion I created using a wind spell to bend light. The magic was normally unusable after dark

due to the lack of sunlight, but the glow from the plasma made it possible. I'd calculated the best place to spread the chaff produced by the Fahr Stone to disperse the plasma and enable my illusion. It didn't matter how fast the hero was if I hid beyond her view.

Got her.

I wasn't dumb enough to say that aloud. I moved silently while hiding my scent and stabbed a knife at Epona's neck from behind as hard as I could.

I heard the dull sound of bone breaking—my wrist. Epona's skin was too hard, sending the entire impact of my full-strength attack back into my hand. My dominant arm was now unusable with that and the other cracked bone.

I wanted to scream from the intense pain, but I didn't have the time. Epona turned around with a backhand blow, and I dodged by a paper-thin margin. Or at least, I thought I did. By the time I realized it had grazed my skin, I was already hurtling backward through the air, as if I were a bullet.

I flew dozens of meters before landing. I was in terrible condition. My clothes were ragged, and my skin torn. The spinning had wrecked my inner ears, and my sense of direction was completely thrown off. I couldn't even stand.

I need to find Epona… Wait. I rolled on instinct, and a crater formed where I'd been a moment earlier. Epona had soared down from the sky to kick me from above. The ground ruptured, and I was tossed into the air again.

I finally regained my sense of direction. *That's going way too far for a duel.* She would have smashed my face in if that kick had connected. If that's how she intended to play it, I'd respond in kind. Fortunately, I'd been knocked a good distance from her. And by miracle or chance, she was standing on the point I designated for my trap.

"Cannon Volley."

I chose Epona's current position as a killing point before the duel. On the way here, I used magic to produce cannons from my Leather Crane Bag and put them in place while running behind Epona. I couldn't hurt her with regular attacks, and there was no time to prepare powerful moves while fighting her. Traps were a different story, though.

We chose a wasteland with a clear view as the site of our duel, but I wasn't so kind as to spend the whole fight engaged on terrain disadvantageous to an assassin. I had been luring her toward the forest, where I could hide and set traps, for the entire duel.

Cannons fired at Epona from all directions with thunderous booms, kicking up a dust cloud. Attacks were stronger when there was less room for the target to escape. Epona knocked me all around during the duel, but the best way to ensure all the force of an attack connected with a target was to strike from all sides with equal strength.

Preparing this trap was difficult. I'd determined the best location for it, but there was no guarantee it would go well. There was limited time to set it without Epona realizing, even with magic to help. I repeatedly compromised and recalculated, and while the location I landed on wasn't ideal, the trap was still plenty lethal. I'd lured Epona to the spot while pretending like she was trouncing me.

"Attacking from all sides with multiple Cannon Strikes upgraded to achieve maximum power. By my estimate, this should exceed Gungnir, but..."

I searched for Epona with a probing spell while still on guard. It didn't take long to find her. She was still moving.

Damn, she's charging right at me.

I tried to react, but my body felt like lead. Was this because of my injuries? No, this was from Haste Bolt. Being a millisecond too slow in this fight could cost me my life.

Epona's nails hardened and sharpened to swords' points, and she stabbed them through my throat... No, she paused just before.

"Darn, I was so close. One more second, and I would've won."

"Yeah, our minute's up."

Epona stopped because we'd reached the time limit.

"I'm surprised. You were able to keep your composure until the end this time," I said.

She kept track of the time down to the second. That would've been impossible if she had lost her mind.

"That was lucky. My vision went red when I saw your Cannon Volley—I could tell it was going to hurt—but getting hit by those bullets actually returned me to my senses... See, I didn't get hurt that badly."

Her left arm hung limp, broken. I succeeded at harming the hero... Although I didn't feel like celebrating, considering it took an attack of Gungnir's level just to break an arm. Epona was more absurd than I thought. I was ready to kill her if necessary, but this reminded me that it would be difficult, even with my new abilities.

Still, I'd say this went well. I confirmed Epona's current strength and proved an even match for her without revealing everything in my arsenal, I thought. Nearly everything I employed in this match was something from my battle against the orc demon. I didn't reveal any new tricks, preferring to keep those for emergencies. Were I not so picky, I would've done even better.

"Sorry about that. I can't hold back when fighting you," I apologized.

"Don't worry. It's already healed. Thanks for going all-out. Anything less would've been unsatisfying, and I feel sharper than I have in ages." Epona waved her arms to show she was okay, including her left one, which had been broken a moment ago.

The injury that nearly cost me my life was already gone. Even my Rapid Recovery skill couldn't keep up with that absurd healing rate. It took all my effort to stand. I didn't look hurt, but I was worn out from boosting my body with magic and the drug. The nerve damage would take a while to heal.

I was unable to dodge Epona's final attack because I'd lost my increased physical strength. I had to expend a lot more effort than anticipated, shortening the time I could maintain my physical strengthening by a few seconds... This didn't happen during my tests. Learning that fighting Epona would push me to this extent made this worthwhile.

"Let's fight again sometime. I want to get stronger. I *have* to."

"Because of that promise?"

"Yeah. But that's not all. I have a skill called Future Calculation, and I don't know why, but it makes my heart pound with fear. It's a vague feeling, but it's like a warning that I'll be in trouble if I remain weak."

That lined up with the private conversation between the goddess and the Puppeteer that the Alam Karla overheard. Under normal circumstances, the hero fought multiple demons and gained strength before fighting the Demon King, but I took those opportunities from her. During the battle with the pig demon—the first we encountered—Epona demonstrated she had what it took to be the strongest hero in history, but she hadn't fought a demon since. I didn't know if she still had that potential.

I need more information.

Epona's weakness wouldn't be an issue if we managed to kill all the demons and prevent the Demon King's resurrection. But if the Demon King returned and the goddess was right that only the hero could defeat them... Then I'd be responsible for leading the world to annihilation instead of salvation.

If that came to be, I would have to take responsibility. I had to protect this world.

Chapter 11 | The Assassin Reunites with the Goddess

I woke up to find myself in a white room.

No, I wasn't awake. This was a dream. I'd been summoned here again. This had happened so many times now that it no longer surprised me.

"It's the goddess again…"

"Heya, it's been a hot second! It's your favorite girl, the goddess! Tee-hee."

"…You changed your personality again. You're just going to confuse me, so please stop."

"Boo. You're as cold as ever. Guess they called you the Icy Assassin for a reason."

"Now, that takes me back."

"I *love* that nickname. It's so edgy! ♪"

I was given many titles in my past life. Only the higher-ups in my organization knew my face and name, causing rumors of a mysterious, skilled assassin to spread through the criminal underworld. There were times when any extremely difficult assassinations with an unknown perpetrator were attributed to me. The embellished nature of the rumors constantly had me exasperated.

"Quit messing around and give me your request."

"I don't have a request. I just wanted to summon you."

"I don't understand… Oh, I guess the summons itself is the message."

"You really are a smart cookie. My resources have been *mega* short recently, so just getting you here took all I had. You have no idea the headache that giving even a little advice would cause me. Spending more than I'm allowed will force me to pull resources from elsewhere, which could end up breaking functions of the world and causing lots of problems!"

That sounded terrifying.

"Are you short on resources because of whatever you were plotting with that demon?"

"Oh come on, you know I can't answer that."

"Because it'll consume resources?"

"Exactly. Interfering with the world comes at a high price… Well, I guess I can tell you one thing, because you already worked it out. I was lying through my teeth when I said you were the only reincarnated soul. But all of the others failed. There's no doubt that you are at the center of the world, and that your actions will decide its fate. Only you can make it that far. As a result, interfering with you demands an absurd amount of resources. Ugh, it makes me want to tear my hair out."

"Sounds like a fine-tuned system."

"It sure is. I can mess with irrelevant nobodies all I want, but it won't have any impact on the world. Meanwhile, meddling with a kid who holds actual influence eats up my resources in a flash. That is to say: You're the world's only hope! I'm counting on you."

The white room crumbled. She really did summon me without a request. I got her message loud and clear anyway.

I woke up for real this time.

"Are you feeling okay, my lord?"

Tarte, who'd already changed into her school uniform, peered at my face with concern. Those clothes suited her very well.

"We've been worried about you. You came back last night all beaten up and then collapsed without a word. I thought you might die," Dia said.

"Epona and I dueled... The hero is ridiculously strong," I responded.

"Well, duh. You know better than anyone that Epona's a superhuman monster."

"You're right about that."

I inspected myself. Rapid Recovery had repaired nearly all of my injuries. My recovery rate was over a hundred times faster than the average person's, which meant that half a day of rest was like three months for anyone else—plenty of time to heal a broken bone. The cracked ones in my rib cage, right wrist, and both arms were fine now. My strained muscles and overworked nerves were back to normal, too.

The problem was...

"This took a lot of effort to make."

...I looked down at the bulletproof vest I wore under my clothes. Its unique, slippery coating deflected weaker slash attacks, and it could survive being hit by a ten-ton truck, thanks to an elastic gel taken from the earth dragon demon's membrane and a frame made to break when overloaded. It was utterly ruined. I might have died if I hadn't been wearing it, but the thought of having to rebuild it was still depressing.

"Don't freak out, Lugh… But that's not all that was broken," Dia said.

"I checked everything while you were asleep, my lord. The barrel of your gun is twisted, your undergarments are ruined… and the amulet prototype you made in case of emergency was broken," Tarte said.

"…I want to hide under the covers and never come out."

I'd skirted most of Epona's direct attacks, but the shock waves they created knocked me off my feet multiple times. Many pieces of equipment I hid under my clothes were destroyed.

"I'll help with repairs!" Tarte declared.

"Guess we don't have much choice. I'll help, too," Dia added.

"I appreciate it. I want to remake your equipment anyway, so I suppose this is good timing. Let's take this opportunity to make upgrades, not just fix," I responded.

I'd made equipment for both the girls, including guns, stab-proof undergarments, and knives made with a special alloy, using knowledge from my past life. To improve on them, I'd need materials surpassing technological possibilities.

Fortunately, I'd defeated multiple demons. Much of a demon's strength came from its body, which could be harvested for materials so excellent they were beyond scientific explanation. Demons turned to blue particles and disappeared when they died, but the most powerful parts of them remained. I've collected and stored the remains of all the demons I've killed.

"Ooh, that sounds fun," Dia said.

"I'm excited," Tarte agreed.

They both looked very interested.

"All right. Let's cut training short today and work on making equipment."

I decided I'd work out the designs in class. It wouldn't be hard for me to multitask.

We held a light training session after school and then moved to my workshop.

"Hey, Lugh. How did you get a workshop as a first-year?" Dia inquired.

"It's a long story. I said I needed one, and the academy provided," I answered.

The academy's headmaster was an ally of the Tuatha Dé clan, and he accommodated me after negotiation.

"Our offensive firepower is sufficient... Well, not quite, but it's getting there. I want to improve our defense. No matter how strong we become, one surprise attack could kill us instantly."

"That's especially true for me. I get really scared sometimes while chanting."

Few mages could use magic in the thick of battle. The reason was because their guard dropped during incantation. Mages used mana to boost their physical abilities, making them a match for a thousand ordinary troops.

Casting a spell meant reciting a formula and investing an amount of mana. A mage couldn't empower themselves and perform magic simultaneously. So while they worked a spell, they were no different from ordinary people. Thus, the safest way for a mage to fight was to rely only on physical strengthening and not cast at all. I didn't let Dia fight that way because she was so adept with magic that the standard rules didn't apply to her. The advantages of using her spells in battle outweighed the risks.

"That's a difficult problem. If you devote more to your physical strengthening, your spells become significantly less powerful, but if you devote more mana to your casting, you become more vulnerable," Tarte said.

"Right? I wish I could wear armor, but... Without physical strengthening, I'd be too slow," Dia agreed.

Good defensive equipment was heavy. That's what the people of this world believed.

"Lugh, make us each one of those vests that breaks to erase impact," Dia requested.

"Sure it's lighter than armor, but it's too heavy for you both. That's why I'm going to make undergarments that are harder than armor and lighter than any clothing... I suppose they might as well be camisoles. Then you can wear them all the time, which is for the best," I explained.

"Ah, we'll be able to wear those every day," Tarte said.

Dia nodded. "Sounds good to me. Like you said yesterday, there's a real chance someone could try to assassinate us at any time."

Making clothing as light as an undergarment while still stab-proof and impact resistant was challenging. Scratch that, impossible—unless you had access to materials that defied science, of course.

"What are you going to make them out of?" Dia asked.

"Do you remember the Puppeteer demon we fought in the holy city?" I said.

"How could we forget?" Dia replied.

Tarte shivered. "He was a very difficult enemy."

"He used telepathic threads when controlling large groups of people, but he needed a physical one to possess formidable targets. I have those here."

These threads remained after the Puppeteer turned to blue particles and disappeared. I performed various tests and discovered they were tougher and lighter than carbon nanotubes. They were only a few micrometers in width, yet could easily lift five tons. It was absurd.

"Can we touch the thread?" Dia asked.

"Sure," I responded.

"It's so light. Even a handful weighs absolutely nothing."

"It's soft, too."

"The Puppeteer used these to transmit thoughts to his targets and control them. Turns out they're equally adept at conducting mana. I can use it to knit light, tough, and magic-compatible camisoles. You'd be hard-pressed to find better defensive equipment."

"I'm excited."

Dia had a big grin on her face, but Tarte turned pale. She realized the problem.

"You're making camisoles with this thread?"

"Yes."

"It's so thin it's invisible. It's terrifying to think how long it would take to knit a camisole... You would need years..."

"Oh, I'm not knitting them by hand. I'm gonna make a loom."

"It's just like you to make one instead of buying one," Dia teased.

"I have no choice. This thread is too strong for an ordinary loom to handle."

Even a scarf took a week to knit with yarn, and the thinner the thread, the more time required. Spinning this thread would take ten times as long, and I didn't even want to think about how many years it might be until I had a camisole.

Tarte sighed. "That's a relief. The first time I knitted you a sweater, Lord Lugh, it took a month."

"I've kept that sweater even after outgrowing it. It's important to me."

"You don't have to do that. You can throw it away."

"No. You made it with love and care. I'd like our kids to wear it one day."

"K-kids...? I'm going to have kids with Lord Lugh...? Heh-heh-heh..."

It was a quality sweater despite it being Tarte's first attempt. She did so well on her first try because of how scrupulous and dedicated she was to the task. I couldn't wear it anymore, but I still treasured it.

"I wish I could do something like that. I've never made you anything," Dia groused.

"What are you talking about? You've made me lots of things."

"I can't remember anything."

"I treasure all the spells we've constructed together. I could never have made them without you. I can't thank you enough."

Dia blushed and laughed. "Yeah, you're lucky to have me. I make spells because I like magic, but it's also for you."

"I know. Thank you... I need to return the favor by making you both defensive equipment that will keep you safe."

I smiled and produced a piece of metal with a spell. Making the loom out of metal was easy—I only had to create each piece in my blueprint. Magic could only fabricate simple shapes, but I could build anything if I conjured the parts individually.

"Is this your blueprint for the loom? Oh, that's what you were drawing in class."

"I don't know how you were able to sketch this. You scare me sometimes, my lord."

My knowledge from my previous life was a constant boon. I acted as many types of people to get close to assassination targets, and I absorbed knowledge on many subjects to ensure convincing performances. That said, I never learned how to make a loom that way. I simply remembered a video. Perhaps it was part of a movie. I wasn't sure. A person operated a loom in the footage, and I reverse engineered the blueprint based on their actions and the functions the machine would require.

"I guess you're gonna put all these parts together once you're done making them. Whoa, there's over a hundred on the blueprint," Dia said.

"That's how complicated this device is," I replied.

Tarte marveled at me. "That's amazing. You're making camisoles by creating the parts necessary for the machine to weave them."

"It's not so unusual. Making a machine to make a machine to make a machine to make a machine that makes the desired product is commonplace," I explained.

Dia groaned. "You're making my head hurt."

That was the fate of the manufacturing industry. At any rate, I expected the three of us to complete the loom by the end of the day. It would take another half a day for me to finish their camisoles.

I'd never seen such beautiful, transparent, and supple thread. This work was for pragmatic pieces of defensive equipment, but they were going to be high-quality camisoles.

The work wasn't too challenging once the loom was built. I wasn't sure building the device for a pair of garments was worthwhile, but it proved to be the right call.

The two finished products were a little larger than necessary because Dia and Tarte were still growing. It wasn't too necessary for Dia, but Tarte's chest could get even larger, hard as that was to believe. I wanted to make extra camisoles if possible, but little of the Puppeteer demon's thread remained. There wasn't enough to spare, considering what I wanted to craft next.

"This is crazy. It's totally see-through," Dia remarked.

"…Wearing this is going to take a lot of courage," Tarte said.

They both blushed as they inspected the finished camisoles.

"The demon's threads are nearly invisible, probably because they needed to catch people off guard… Weaving it together resulted in transparent fabric."

Transparent thread was an incredible material. See-through camisoles existed in my old world, of course, but they were created with thin thread and weaving that left many gaps. The material itself wasn't see-through. A genuinely transparent item of clothing, one created with no spaces, could function as defensive equipment. Such a thing was unthinkable in my old world, though.

Dia put a hand to her chin. "Can you color these? That would make them even nicer."

"I tried to dye them because I was worried about the transparency, too, but the color wouldn't stick," I answered.

I applied a red dye to one of the camisoles to demonstrate, and it slid right off. I'd attempted several methods to color the garments, including soaking them in paint and baking the paint into them, but all ended in failure.

"Huh. Well, guess it's not possible. We'll be wearing them under our clothes, so it doesn't really matter," Dia said.

"Um, that's fine for me, but in your case..." Tarte trailed off.

Dia's ears turned red. "Don't say that in front of Lugh!"

"S-sorry."

I had an idea of what this was about. Camisoles were supposed to be worn above underwear. Tarte had a developed chest and needed to wear a bra, but Dia could get by with just a camisole. Wearing a transparent camisole over her bare skin wasn't going to work, however.

"How about this? I'll use my Natural You connections to find you some small and cute underwear," I suggested.

Dia had a chest. It was growing little by little, and she'd probably reach a B cup before long. She didn't need a bra, but I thought it'd be better for her to have one. I'd have Maha choose something soft and comfortable to wear.

"Mind your own business. I *have* bras, for your information! I just don't use them 'cause they're a pain. It's much easier to wear a camisole."

Dia could be surprisingly lazy when it came to anything other than magic. She could play the perfect noble lady in public settings with exquisite etiquette that befitted her birth, but she took it easy in her private life wherever she could. It was just like her to wear a thick camisole over her bare skin.

"I know you do, but the fabric is low quality, and they don't fit you right... And uh, I don't think you've noticed, but you are growing. You should take this chance to buy something nice."

"Wait, really?! Wow..."

I broached the topic nervously because of its delicate nature, but Dia shamelessly rubbed her chest in front of us.

"I think they have grown... I'd given up hope! Yep, you can buy me underwear, Lugh. I'll tell you my size later."

"You amaze me, Lady Dia..." Tarte's praise was likely meant for Dia's boldness, not the increase in her chest size.

"You got it," I responded.

Viekones grew and aged slowly. That's why my mom still looked young despite being in her late thirties, and Dia came from the same bloodline. She was turning seventeen soon, but her physical age was fourteen or fifteen. There was a chance she would keep growing.

"Also...," Dia began.

"What is it?"

"Remember those fake boobs we used for my disguise? I want those, too!"

"Don't even think about it. Once you start exaggerating your appearance like that, you'll never be able to stop."

"I don't like the sound of that, but..."

Dia was asking for a padded bra. I made one for her as part of a disguise when we sneaked into a party in the royal capital. I had a collection of tools for altering appearance, and I was able to make the large chest look perfectly natural on her. I was sure she could use it to fool everyone into thinking her breasts were large. The

problem was that she couldn't just claim her bust shrank one day. There were two choices: wear the fake chest for the rest of her life or admit to using padding. It was a curse.

"Then forget it."

"You're mean."

"I'm not saying it to be cruel... Anyway, let's call it there for today. You two can go back without me."

"You're staying here?"

"I prioritized your equipment, so I'm not done repairing my bulletproof vest. Once it's done, I'll head back to the dorm."

"You should've made a camisole for yourself, too. It's more comfortable."

"I'm stronger than you two, so I want the added defense of a heavier piece of gear."

The camisoles weren't much different from the vest when up against slashing attacks, but only a vest could achieve the level of impact resistance I wanted. That vest was my lifeline—I always wore it under my clothes.

Now that I was a saint, I'd be the target of great jealousy. Some nobles would try to eliminate me if they couldn't bring me under their influence. I didn't want to die now that I lived as a person instead of a weapon. I'd finally found happiness.

"I'd offer to help...but I'll only be in the way. See you later," Dia bid.

"I'll prepare supper for you," Tarte added.

They both held their camisoles to their chests and left. Knowing they'd wear those eased my fears, if only somewhat.

I hadn't forgotten about myself while working on those two garments. Dia and Tarte just had a higher chance of becoming targets than I did. When trying to take down a formidable opponent, it was common practice to go after their loved ones. That's why I prioritized their safety over mine. No matter the world, the malice hidden within everyday people was more terrifying than anything.

"Okay, one final push."

I had a plan to experiment with the Puppeteer demon's thread to improve my bulletproof vest.

I lost track of time as I worked on improving the vest and ended up returning to the dorm in the middle of the night. It was well past Dia and Tarte's usual bedtime. And yet...

"Welcome back, my lord."

"What took you so long?"

...they'd both waited up for me. The girls were wearing comfortable nightgowns that we'd bought in Milteu, which they slept in regularly because of how soft and loose-fitting they were.

"You could've just gone to bed," I said.

Dia shook her head. "I would've felt guilty... And I have something for you. I couldn't help with the defensive equipment, but it felt wrong to relax while you worked, so I made a new spell."

I took the piece of paper Dia offered me and read the formula written on it.

"Huh. This is interesting. Did you come up with this on your own?" I asked.

"I wouldn't be worthy of being called a genius if I let you do everything," Dia replied.

I was truly surprised. She didn't have the advantage of being reincarnated like me; it was incredible that she came up with this alone. The spell had limited use, but it could turn a situation around when one was backed into a corner.

"I can't make anything like that, so I put extra effort into my cleaning and cooking," Tarte said.

I nodded. "Thank you. I overtaxed my brain, so I'm craving something sweet."

Improving the vest was difficult, and my brain wanted glucose. I took a bite of a cupcake Tarte had made. The sweetness suited my tastes perfectly, as was always the case. Tarte had even adjusted the recipe, using soy milk instead of cow's milk to make the cupcake lighter because it was a late-night snack.

Tarte was hardly the best cook in the world. I was more skilled than she was. But no one understood my tastes the way she did— not even me. That was because every meal she made since entering my service was for me.

"We have one more gift for you," Dia announced.

"Um, Lady Dia, are we really doing that? I will do my best if it makes Lord Lugh happy, but...," Tarte said.

"It absolutely will. Lugh may not look it at first glance, but he's a total perv. He just likes to play it cool."

"Ouch. Wording, Dia."

Unfortunately, I couldn't deny it. Becoming more human was my goal after reincarnation, so I wanted to give in to my budding desires on occasion. Was there anything wrong with that?

"If you say so. Here we go!" Tarte declared.

Dia and Tarte both dropped their nightgowns, stripping to nothing but their underwear. Actually, no—they were wearing the transparent camisoles as well. Tarte's underwear was simple, but the elaborate design of Dia's drew my attention.

I'd never seen the underwear Dia was wearing before. Judging by its design, it wasn't fit for everyday use. A careless wash would ruin it. That meant it was made for...other purposes. I struggled to imagine Dia purchasing this. I suspected my mother's involvement.

"What do you think?" asked Dia. "I thought I would treat you to a look at me in this camisole. Isn't it cute?"

"Urgh, I'm so embarrassed," Tarte groaned.

"It's strange. You look sexier with the transparent camisoles than you would with your underwear alone," I observed.

"Don't analyze us like that, my lord!"

I only made the camisoles to protect them, but they did look really nice. The sight of Dia and Tarte in them appealed to my base instincts.

"Thanks. I feel totally refreshed," I said.

"Is that all?" Dia asked.

"No. I'm a man. I can't look at you in those outfits and not be aroused. But it's late, and it'd be rude to invite one of you to bed when all three of us are here."

I had a pubescent body, and Dia and Tarte were my adorable fiancées. Seeing them this way filled me with desire. However, taking one of them would be rude, and I'd have to be really shameless to request that both girls join me.

"Then I'll ask. Are you opposed to that?"

"No, it'd make me happy, but—"

"Then let's go to my room."

"Wha—huh—I—huh?" Tarte panicked.

Dia smiled at her, taking my hand. "Tarte, I'll hog Lugh forever if you don't say what you want. Words don't seem to be getting through, so I'm going to bully you like this until you learn to speak up."

I smiled wryly. Dia really was an excellent big sister. Fixing Tarte's passivity demanded drastic measures.

Dia and I went into her room, leaving Tarte behind, looking like a child whose toy was taken. It had been a long time since I'd made love to Dia.

Today was a holiday, meaning we had no classes. I took advantage of my free time by staying in my room and analyzing all the traces of Naoise that my information network collected. I desperately hoped to find him.

Naoise was the heir to one of the four major dukedoms, so his disappearance became quite a scandal. He'd vanished before, but always made arrangements to ensure that no one took issue with his absence. This time he didn't bother. I inferred that meant he didn't plan to come back.

"I hope House Romalung has some info…"

Nevan had taken my advice and begun searching for Naoise using House Romalung's operatives. Dad had been dispatched for the same purpose. He was among the best assassins in the country—no one was more qualified for the job than he was.

A carrier pigeon arrived just as I reached a stopping point.

"A letter from Dad…"

The bird was a special breed raised by the Tuatha Dé clan. It was tougher and flew faster than ordinary carrier pigeons. I took the letter and deciphered the coded message.

"…Talk about ominous."

Dad's message sounded like a will. It told me where documents important to House Tuatha Dé were stored and that he'd affixed his seal to the ones necessary for me to succeed him. He also shared the whereabouts of a book containing Tuatha Dé secrets he'd yet to teach me, instructed me about inheriting the duties of a feudal lord, and asked that I look after my mom and unborn sister. And finally...

"I'm surprised Dad would joke like this... No, he's serious."

...he said that if Mom tried to remarry after his death, he wanted me to oppose it as her son and meticulously obstruct any potential suitors. A part of me thought it'd be better for Dad to wish Mom happiness, but I guess that was just how much he loved her. He wanted to keep her for himself, even in death. I understood where he was coming from—the notion of Dia remarrying hurt my heart.

"Sending this letter means he feels he might die on this job."

I was the reason he had this assignment. On the off chance that anything happened, I would swear to carry out the contents of this will to the letter. I didn't have to worry about my mom remarrying. Knowing her, she'd never take another husband.

I finished analyzing the information.

"It's no use. I still have no idea where Naoise is. There's one thing I'm worried about, though. The writing of my intelligence agent in Gephis feels a little different."

My operatives recorded themselves reading written reports when contacting me over the telecommunications network. I gathered these audio logs and listened to them. The voice undoubtedly belonged to the agent deployed in the Gephis domain, but something was off about their wording... Almost as though they were being forced to read a document prepared by someone else.

I trusted my intelligence agents but remained aware that an

enemy could capture them. Thus, I made sure to memorize their voices and writing habits.

Naoise's family rules the Gephis domain. There's no way this irregularity is a coincidence.

What if Mina captured my operative and forced them to read false reports?

I gave each of my agents a portable communication device, but none of them would give away the location of a base unit... My telecommunications network should be safe. Still, it's best to assume all information shared on the network, especially on open channels, will be heard by the enemy.

I wondered if I should head to Gephis, but I decided against that. Information was the priority. That domain was dangerous territory now, and I had to be prepared. Nevan surely understood that as well as I did, which meant that House Romalung had likely performed a thorough investigation already.

When I visited Nevan, she suggested we move to a terrace in the courtyard, offering tea upon our arrival. She lived in the S-class dorm like I did, so I could drop by whenever I wanted. The Alam Karla had finally been deemed safe the other day, which allowed Nevan to return to the academy.

"I'm flattered by the visit, Sir Lugh, but is it not a bit early to creep into a girl's bedroom?"

"This is no time for jokes... My intelligence agent in the Gephis domain assigned to the telecommunications network has been captured."

"Interesting... I wonder how that happened."

"What's going on in Gephis? Tell me everything you know."

"I could do that, but I have no obligation to tell you anything for free."

"I suspect that House Romalung is at fault for information on my intelligence agents leaking."

"That's possible. But do you have proof?"

I promised to let Duke Romalung use my telecommunications network as part of our deal, and I passed him information about my agents so he could access it. I doubted my operative would have been discovered otherwise.

"No, but...there's value enough in knowing that something has happened to one of my people. I want compensation."

"I suppose you're right. Very well. Let's see, where should I start? Famous knights in the Gephis domain have been disappearing lately. The first to vanish were those of the Gephis Ducal Guard. Each one of them is an elite, as you would expect of knights in the employ of one of the four great dukedoms. They are the strongest order in this kingdom and beyond—House Romalung excluded, of course. Their vanishing is concerning."

The knights of the Gephis Ducal Guard were strong. Even I would struggle against them in a one-on-one sword fight. They were one of the big three orders in Alvan.

"...I didn't hear anything about that. I should assume my agent has been a puppet for a while now."

"That must be the case. Even House Romalung only learned of this yesterday in a report from your father."

"Don't be absurd. I'm sure there are Romalung agents in Gephis. Undoubtedly, they sent a carrier pigeon immediately after learning of the knights' disappearance."

"You're right. However, our agents have become puppets of the enemy as well. They've made fools of us all."

I couldn't believe my ears. My agent's capture was shocking, but it didn't totally shock me. Using the telecommunications network gave my operatives a massive advantage, and I chose them from a qualified group of knights who idolized me—espionage was not their specialty. That was not true of House Romalung's agents, though. They were highly trained, with an aptitude for intelligence. It was difficult to imagine them getting caught.

"I'm sure House Romalung sent several of its most elite agents. Are you suggesting they were all rounded up with no time to report their abduction? And that they failed to commit suicide, allowing the enemy to use them to send false information? I don't believe it. Are you sure about this?"

"I doubted it at first, too, but unfortunately, we've found evidence to confirm your father's report. I offer you my deepest apologies. I challenged your accusation, but considering the situation and the timing of your agent's capture, it's likely that House Romalung is at fault for the information leak."

Nevan bowed, graceful even in apology. The situation was even worse than I thought.

"Someone has conquered the Gephis domain. Their total control over information shows that their takeover is complete. Gephis is not a simple hideout for the enemy—the entire region should be considered subject to their whims. We need to take immediate—"

I stopped talking when Nevan and I both sensed a presence. We stood, strengthened ourselves with all our mana, and reached for our weapons.

"Ha-ha-ha, you two never cease to impress. I can see why that boy is so jealous. I'm tempted to eat you both and add you to my collection."

A voluptuous woman appeared. She had dark skin and vertical irises like a serpent's. It was Mina, the snake demon with a love for human culture, my supposed ally.

"...I see you've dropped the human act," I said.

Mina disguised herself as a noble to infiltrate aristocratic society, and she always maintained human form to keep up the ruse. Now, however, she exposed her snake eyes and tail, flaunting her overwhelming power. *Not suited for combat, my ass. She's stronger than any demon I've fought yet.*

"I have no need to conceal myself any longer. You two guessed correctly—I'm going to use what I've conquered to make this country mine," Mina responded.

"Are you talking about the Gephis domain? The missing knights are already monsters, then?"

"Hee-hee, I'm just getting started. My little Naoise is going to lead my adorable children and conquer this nation's domains one by one. You humans are powerless to resist."

House Gephis was the only family in the kingdom powerful enough to challenge House Romalung. If Mina had captured its elite knights and increased their strength by turning them into snake people, she really stood a chance at taking over.

"What happened to enjoying human culture?"

"Oh, Lugh. I can enjoy human culture just fine after conquering the world. I will become the Demon King and rule the world, not destroy it. I won't kill anyone who surrenders to me."

Something had changed for Mina. She had me eliminate the other demons competing to become the Demon King because her strength supposedly paled in comparison to theirs. There were still other demons left, but something had happened to change her mind.

"Did you come here to tell us that?"

"Yes. It may be over now, but we had an alliance. I felt obligated to inform you that I'm moving on. Thank you very much for eliminating those pesky rivals of mine. You've done great work for me," Mina said.

"You're very welcome," I responded with a smile, preparing to kill her. I could keep the damage to a minimum if I took her out now. The problem was, I'd brought only minimal weaponry to avoid putting Nevan on edge. Dia's absence made this a challenge as well. The chances of me successfully hitting Mina with Demonkiller *and* inflicting a mortal wound were very low.

"I have one other purpose for visiting. I thought I'd let you know my adorable little Naoise's request."

Mina disappeared. She hadn't moved so quickly that my eyes couldn't follow. Rather, her presence vanished entirely, as though she'd teleported. She next appeared before Nevan. This must have been a special ability of hers.

Mina put a finger under Nevan's chin and lifted her face. "Hee-hee, that boy had the gall to give me a condition... He told me to leave you alive. It would be *so* much fun to torment such a beautiful girl."

Nevan silently retaliated with a high kick. It was an impressive attack, strong enough to break an experienced knight's neck, but Mina easily caught the blow.

"Oh dear, it's improper for a girl to lift her legs like that... I promised not to hurt you, but this is self-defense. It's hardly my fault."

"Gah!"

Nevan attempted to free her captured limb by twisting it, but Mina threw her before she could. Nevan crashed into a brick wall and fell limply to the ground.

"That strength... You're not already the Demon King, are you?" I asked.

Mina laughed. "Hmm-hmm-hmm, you're way off. I merely obtained the fodder you found for me."

"No way... You ate the Fruit of Life...?"

"You clearly took great pains to hide and seal it, but your efforts were a waste. You can't keep anything from me. I have more than monsters in my employ—I also share the senses of every snake in the world. You're an assassin, aren't you? You're doing your best as a human, but snakes are assassins from birth. You can't possibly best them."

Snakes could certainly be considered nature's assassins. Instead of relying on eyesight, they observed the world with pit organs on their heads that detected infrared radiation from warm bodies. No one could eliminate body heat, no matter how skilled they were at avoiding detection. Slithering was also much quieter than walking, and their low point of vision helped them surprise prey. Furthermore, their high adaptability meant they could live anywhere. If Mina truly did share the vision of all serpents, it would be impossible to get anything by her.

"Well, congrats on taking one step toward becoming the Demon King. But you need at least three Fruits of Life, right? Have you worked out how to get the other two?"

Just one Fruit of Life granted her astronomical strength. If she intended to become the Demon King, I had no choice but to kill her now.

"Yes, the second will be harvested shortly. The boy is using his knights to round up his own citizens and make one for me. I'll obtain the third soon after. Hmm-hmm-hmm, ha-ha-ha!"

I couldn't believe it. I was going to be the lord of the Tuatha Dé domain one day, so I knew what it was like to have subjects. How could a lord, who was supposed to protect his people, sacrifice them to a demon? I couldn't allow it.

I tried to regain my composure and, in an attempt to kill Mina immediately, drew my pistol and shot three times. All three bullets bounced off her skin. The sight made me recall my recent duel with Epona. Defeating Mina would be similarly difficult.

"Is that any way to treat a lady? I have no intention of attacking you. However, I only spared the girl because little Naoise insisted. I don't want to kill you, Lugh. You've worked so hard for me. Don't you think we could continue to make a great team?" Mina asked.

"You have no shame. You intended to betray me from the beginning, once you obtained the power you sought," I responded.

"I could say the same of you."

She was right. This was my fault for letting her betray me first.

"I have one warning for you. Don't get in my way if you value your life. I'll leave you alone if you keep to yourself. Run and never look back, and you won't have to die."

"And if I do get in your way?"

"I'll capture you and make you my pet. Both of you. You'll be much better toys than the boy." Mina disappeared.

This was bad. Really bad. Still, I had options. There was no way in hell I could run. If I did, Mina would conquer the kingdom, which meant the Tuatha Dé domain's ruin. I wouldn't abandon the place I loved.

I treated Nevan's injuries and carried her to her bed. She had broken bones and multiple organ contusions, but fortunately, her life was not in danger. Mina could've easily killed her. I was sure she only spared her life because of her promise to Naoise.

Nevan woke up. "...I'm alive."

"The demon spared you. You should thank Naoise."

"Like hell I'd thank him. It's his fault we're in this mess."

I couldn't deny that. Mina likely had captured Gephis, thanks to her connection to Naoise.

"We need to act fast," I said.

"Agreed. We can't let her make a second Fruit of Life. If she succeeds, she'll quickly invade another domain and obtain a third," Nevan responded.

"...You were conscious during that conversation?"

"I fought hard to stay awake until the demon left."

"Huh."

"I'm...in no condition to fight."

"No, you aren't."

Mina held back when she attacked, and Nevan limited her injuries with her incredible reflexes, but she was going to be out of commission for a while.

"I apologize, but may I request a favor of you?" she asked.

"Depends on the favor," I answered.

"Please kill that boy. It's the only way to save him. No matter how we manipulate information about the incident, there will be no defending his attempt to slaughter his people. Killing him on the battlefield is for the best."

"That's for sure."

"Protecting the common folk is the duty of the aristocracy. Not even giving up his life can atone for this crime."

Naoise had become an enemy of the Alvanian Kingdom and humanity. Even if he cut ties with Mina right now, it was too late. Rejoining human society was impossible. All I could do for him was end his life.

"Do you have any idea why Naoise did this?" I asked.

"More or less. He's always struggled with an inferiority complex. There's something I want you to tell that idiot if you find him." Nevan looked vulnerable, more like a sister concerned for her brother than the masterpiece of humanity she always projected herself as.

"I'll tell him, I promise."

"I don't mind if you say it after you kill him. Don't pass up a chance to assassinate him just to deliver my message."

The Tuatha Dé were assassins by trade. An ideal assassination meant delivering a lethal blow before your target noticed you. There was no room for talking. If I had a chance to relay Nevan's words, then I'd have already messed up.

"That's the plan."

"I expected no less. Normally, we would have the royal family issue this job, but this is an emergency. Please forgive me for skipping formal procedures." Nevan's expression returned to one befitting a lady of House Romalung. "By the name of House

Romalung, one of the four major dukedoms, in place of the royal family, I order you to wield your Tuatha Dé blade for the sake of the Alvanian Kingdom. Remove Naoise Gephis, who has become a lesion plaguing this land."

This was the language used when giving the Tuatha Dé clan a target. The order instructed us to kill for the benefit of the kingdom.

"I recognize that Naoise Gephis is a lesion harming the kingdom. On my pride as a Tuatha Dé, I will remove him."

Rather than blindly following orders, we accepted jobs only after confirming with our own eyes and ears that the assassination was in the kingdom's best interest. That was how Tuatha Dé assassins operated.

There was no backing out after agreeing. Over the generations, my family had taken hundreds, if not thousands, of jobs. And none of us went back on our word.

I contacted Duke Romalung immediately after leaving Nevan to tell him of his daughter's injuries and the present situation. He sent carrier pigeons across the kingdom to spread the news that a demon had conquered the Gephis domain and that Naoise had sold his soul and aided in the attack. Naoise no longer had a place in this kingdom. Duke Romalung also gave an official order for me to kill Naoise as a Holy Knight.

I'm going to miss Dia and Tarte on this operation. I was acting alone, so I left my assistants behind. The job required infiltrating the Gephis domain and assassinating Naoise on a battlefield teeming with enemies. There was no way we could overpower an entire army, so it made more sense to go solo and prioritize stealth. I also didn't expect to fight Mina, so I didn't need Dia to use Demonkiller.

A hang glider would have been too conspicuous, so I sprinted along a road on a dark, moonless night. I was already close to the Gephis domain. *Never thought I'd see the day we use the hero as a decoy.* That was Epona's role in this operation. She was charging directly into the city to rampage through the knights-turned-snake-monsters.

The hope was that this would draw out Mina so Epona could fight her. That didn't mean the hero was a decoy, though. She was going to take out a good chunk of House Gephis's powerful knights, and if she happened to lure out Naoise, she could just kill him herself. If she didn't, her actions would buy me time to take care of it.

I'm surprised those corrupt politicians in the capital allowed Epona to participate. The hero had been stuck in the royal capital from nearly the moment she obtained her powers. Demons targeted cities with large populations to create Fruits of Life, which placed the royal capital in danger. Those in power in the capital wanted the hero close by to protect themselves.

I guess they realized that wasn't going to fly this time. The Gephis domain stood near the royal capital and many regions ruled by powerful nobles. It also had the strongest order of knights in the kingdom, and if they started wreaking havoc with the might of a demon to help, no one would be able to stop them. The cowards in the capital had no choice but to send their precious hero to prevent that.

I hadn't expected to work solely with Epona, but it was the

best choice for a fast surprise attack. No one else would be able to keep up with us, and any delay was more time for Naoise to kill the Gephis domain's citizens and produce a Fruit of Life.

I climbed onto high ground and, with self-made binoculars, studied Geil, the large city in the center of the Gephis domain.

"What a horrible sight."

Half-serpent knights butchered the citizens they'd sworn to protect, and the souls of the dead gathered together. They were in the process of creating the Fruit of Life, which was produced by bundling and distorting human souls. About ten thousand souls were needed.

By my estimate, over three thousand people were already dead. Killing all the fleeing people seemed to be a time-consuming process. Judging by the rate at which they were progressing, the slaughter likely began a few hours ago.

This actually would have been easier if everyone was already dead. Were that the case, I would've carpet-bombed the city with Gungnir, which caused great destruction for a small amount of mana. Gungnir was a spell that lifted a spear thousands of kilometers into the air using reverse gravity before letting it fall back to the ground, creating force four hundred times more powerful than a large-caliber tank gun. Gravity gave it incredible power for a low drain on my magical power.

I could've wiped out the snake people by dropping dozens of those god spears. There was no safer and more efficient method. But wiping out the city wasn't an option. *There are still over ten thousand people in the city, though. Dad could be among them.* No matter how efficient it was, I couldn't bring myself to eradicate the enemy if it meant killing so many, and potentially my dad as well.

I probably would have done it in my old life. Considering the pros and cons, it was obviously the best choice. Infiltrating a city packed with monsters to kill Naoise would take some real acrobatics. My chances of success weren't high, and if I failed, the people of Geil would die anyway. If killing everyone in this city would save the country, there was no reason to hesitate. However...

That's not how Lugh Tuatha Dé operates. It was naive. Irrational. Still, I'd follow my heart. That was the kind of person I'd become.

◇

The chaos of mass slaughter made entering Geil easy. I dressed as a normal citizen, used a mask to disguise my face, and limited my mana output to a minimum.

The city was like hell on Earth. That much was clear from a distance but even more appalling up close. The knights who swore to protect people were killing everyone they got their hands on, and the city wall built to keep enemies out had become a cage.

There was a great variety among the knights. Some were snakes from the neck up, others had scales all over their bodies, and a few looked perfectly human except for their tongues. Behaviors differed as well—some delighted in the slaughter, while others cried and apologized as they killed. I even saw a few murder innocents with no emotion whatsoever. Perhaps that spoke to a quality I could take advantage of.

I followed the knights' chain of command. *Even now, they remain knights who follow orders from a superior.* That made this easy.

Knights abided by a firm chain of command. An order typically consisted of battalions composed of smaller companies, which were further divided into platoons of four knights each. Orders came from the top down. Thus, I could study a platoon to discern its captain, then observe the captains to find the company leader, and keep moving up the chain. Naoise was at the top. Mina had installed herself as the ruler of the Gephis domain, but the army followed Naoise.

These knights are skilled as can be. Their strict adherence to regulations will make this a cinch.

Knights differed in every domain. Typically, poorly trained knights were completely disorganized in battle and made independent decisions. Knights were more formidable the more organized they were, but that orderliness aided me.

I moved among the fleeing citizens and traced the chain of command. *Finding Naoise shouldn't take too long... Wait, what's that insane surge of mana coming from the east?!*

An explosion shook the ground. I looked east toward the immense outpouring of mana and saw that a massive chunk of the city wall was gone. No longer trapped, the panicked citizens flooded toward the broken wall, attempting to escape. The knights moved in a regimented manner to block their path, but a ferocious wind knocked them away.

"Don't worry, everyone. I am the hero, Epona, and I have come to put a stop to this evil!"

Epona had arrived... Quicker than I expected, too. I saved time on the journey by using a hang glider to take a shortcut, yet she arrived only an hour after.

The hero's arrival gave people hope. They cried tears of joy, prayed, and cheered. Epona lived up to her title.

She immediately set to work. The knights-turned-snake-monsters were like flies before a hurricane. Some of them were as strong as I was, but they didn't have a chance. This was the hero—a superhuman monster. She must have held back during our duel.

However, as I marveled at Epona's strength, something sent her flying. I was a bit surprised—Mina had appeared, not Naoise.

"You're early, Lord Hero. I can't have you breaking any more of my cute little toys. You face me now," the snake demon declared.

"You're the one responsible for all this, huh? I'm going to kill you."

The enormously powerful hero clashed with the equally formidable snake demon. I was more than happy about this upset in my plan. Epona had drawn the attention of the most powerful piece on the board, giving me the perfect opportunity to do my job.

It was time to assassinate Naoise, my friend who'd become an enemy of humanity.

Epona and Mina's battle was stunning. It was far beyond human capability. The mere sounds and the way they lit up the sky made it feel like the end of the world.

I'd heard that the latest hero's growth was stunted from lack of practice, but I nearly laughed at that idea now. *Epona claimed she got weaker, but she's still absurdly strong. She clearly doesn't need my help. I'd only get in her way.*

The sound of her battle with Mina grew steadily more distant. They were moving away from the city. The old Epona would've entered a blind rage once she loosed her power and trampled friend and foe alike. Thankfully, she was able to keep her head enough to spare the city. Clearly, she'd made an effort to improve her self-control.

I returned to following the chain of command and spotted something. *A sign from Dad.* The Tuatha Dé clan typically performed jobs with as few people as possible, but we cooperated with others when the situation called for it. There was a scratch on a house that looked perfectly natural but was actually part of a code my family used to communicate secretly on the scene. It told me to meet up and pointed to the next sign, which in turn would lead me to the next. This formed a trail that would take me to my dad.

I need to make the right choice. If I interrupted my search for Naoise to meet up with Dad, I'd have to start over with tracing the chain of command. I couldn't imagine Epona losing to Mina, but that didn't mean I could waste time.

After some consideration, I made my decision. *I'll prioritize meeting with Dad.* Cian Tuatha Dé was considered the strongest Tuatha Dé in history until I claimed the title. He had to know what taking up my time in this situation meant, yet he ordered me to find him anyway. He probably knew something I didn't and judged that information to be critical.

My choice was based on trust in my father.

The signs led me to an abandoned building in a slum. I rapped on the door in the special Tuatha Dé style. It sounded like a normal knock, but we used the pitch and the intervals between each hit to announce that we were friend and not foe. Specific patterns could even convey our present situation.

A sound came from inside, the response bidding me enter. Before I did so, I checked to make sure no one was watching me—including snakes. There were three people in the room. The first was Dad, the second was a muscular man with a splendid mustache, and the third was the corpse of a man who'd become a snake monster.

"Thank you for coming, son," Dad said.

"I'm glad you're safe... Though I notice you're hurt," I responded.

Dad had lost his right arm. My nose caught the acrid scent of burned flesh. He'd likely burned his wound to close it and stop the bleeding because there was no time for a better treatment. There was no way to reconnect the limb now.

"This is what I get for forgetting that killing is my specialty, not saving people."

Dad smiled despite his injury. Even now, he maintained his pleasant manner. By stark contrast, the middle-aged man beside him cowered in an apparent mental breakdown. I recognized him.

"I'm amazed you're still human... Duke Gephis."

He was Naoise's father and the lord of this domain. I met him once at a meeting. I assumed he was the first person Mina would want to make into her puppet.

"Why...? Why did this happen...? I acknowledged you as my son, Naoise, despite your impure blood... I tolerated your imperfections... Ugh...," he muttered deliriously.

Dad spoke for him. "Turning Duke Gephis would have caused him to grow snakelike features. Dukes have many duties that take them outside their domain, and Mina and Naoise wanted to operate in secret until they began the slaughter. They threatened him to keep silent on what was happening here."

That made sense. They needed a human to interact with the other leaders of the kingdom, so they left Duke Gephis unharmed and threatened him to do their bidding.

"How long has the snake demon had control of the city?" I asked.

"I don't know exactly. At least a month. She started with House Gephis and corrupted the city from there. There was no stopping her once Naoise turned. The turmoil with you and the Alamite Church also served as a useful distraction," Dad explained.

Mina and Naoise had planned this very carefully... I was stunned that they'd seized control of the Gephis domain without my or House Romalung's intelligence agents noticing. Perhaps I'd underestimated Naoise's capabilities.

"Moving on... Don't tell me you called me here to save this guy," I said.

"Heavens no. Do I look like that much of a fool? His life is worthless," Dad said, balking.

Duke Gephis was stunned. Despite his position, his fate was irrelevant at this point. The corrupted knights answered only to Mina and Naoise, and the duke had long since lost the people's trust. They wouldn't listen to him, either. His only use was to take responsibility and give himself up as an example once this was over.

"I interrupted your mission because there is something you need to know. Everything that is happening here—including the snake demon's fight with Epona and the slaughter of the citizens— is a decoy."

"...I see. Naoise is already heading for another city with a force of soldiers, then?"

"That's right. They have been quite wary of you and Epona. Their plan is to cause commotion to pin you both down in the Gephis domain and use that opportunity to create a Fruit of Life elsewhere. Consuming that Fruit of Life will give Mina power surpassing the hero's. She's fighting Epona to buy time. Naoise also anticipated that you'd try to find him through the chain of command. Doing so will lead you to a former commander of the Ducal Guard, not to him."

I shuddered. Had I ignored Dad's sign, my efforts would've been wasted, giving Naoise time to butcher another city and return with the spoils, creating a monster beyond the hero. We would've been finished.

"One thing doesn't make sense to me. How did Naoise lead a force that large out of the city without being detected?" I asked.

"By using a tunnel created by snake monsters," Dad said.

I recalled the giant serpent I rode on the way to Mina's estate. It was definitely big enough to burrow a tunnel and transport passengers at high speeds.

"Thank you, Dad. I should still be able to catch Naoise." That was a close call. Without Dad here, I would've definitely failed to stop Naoise and Mina. There was one thing I was curious about, though. "How did you learn all this?"

"He told me," Dad said, pointing at the corpse of the snake man. "He was the commander of the Gephis Ducal Guard. He maintained his sense of self even after becoming a monster and fought Mina's control."

"He learned of their plan because they believed he was dominated."

"Exactly. He resisted control, told me everything he knew, and died begging me to take care of his lord. His brain couldn't handle the fight to maintain free will. He was a loyal subject. I liberated him from pain as repayment. That was the only reward he wanted."

A demon's rule was not so easily resisted. This man protected his lord while enduring tremendous agony. It must have been terrifying for him. His knightly fortitude deserved praise.

"The entrance to the underground tunnel is in this building. The commander told me that, too."

"Thanks. I'll take care of the rest. But first, I have a request for you: Don't die. I'm not ready to carry all of Tuatha Dé by myself. And also, I'd rather die than try to prevent Mom from remarrying."

"Hmm. Well, I suppose that leaves me with no choice but to make it home. You stay alive, too. Losing you would destroy Esri, and you can't abandon your fiancées."

"You're right." That was the last thing I said before I left.

I ran as fast as I could. It was going to be close, but I'd make it. Dad saved me from certain defeat. Now it was time to turn things around. I had to stop Naoise from committing mass murder and from creating a Fruit of Life.

The spacious underground tunnel ran directly under the lord's estate. I used a spell to fly through it. I was also using magic created for covert operations, including one spell that bent light with a layer of wind to conceal myself and others that masked my body heat and scent. I couldn't have the enemy notice my approach.

They've been playing me like a fiddle this whole time. I'm not going to botch my first chance to catch them off guard. Some snakes sensed vibration, which meant they would notice footsteps. I also needed to account for heat, vision, and smell. All the spells I cast lowered my speed, but moving stealthily was paramount.

After twenty kilometers, I emerged aboveground, lifted myself high into the air, and released the taxing spells I used to hide. I then produced a hang glider from my Leather Crane Bag; they weren't going to sense the vibration from this elevation.

"Well, this is gonna be easy."

I strengthened my Tuatha Dé eyes with mana to improve my vision from the sky, but that was hardly necessary. The tracks left by Naoise's giant snake monsters as they slithered for their destination were clearly visible, even from the sky.

"Time to go all-out."

I didn't have to worry about avoiding detection at this height, which enabled me to devote all my mana to movement. I used wind magic to produce a cowl that minimized air resistance and to summon a gust that propelled me from behind. I could have moved significantly faster with an explosive spell, but the noise would give me away. I took care not to cross the sound barrier for the same reason.

I didn't care how fast those snakes moved. They couldn't escape aerial pursuit.

These tracks look fifteen minutes old. Considering the direction and the need for ten thousand souls to create a Fruit of Life...they're headed for Faryl, the largest city in the Distore domain. There's no doubt about it.

Faryl was thirty kilometers away. I needed to hurry.

I caught up to Naoise and his force of soldiers three minutes later. It was a horrifying procession formed of ten giant serpents like the one I rode to Mina's estate. Each carried ten snake people, for a total of one hundred soldiers, every one of them a mage. Only House Gephis or House Romalung could assemble such a force. Tuatha Dé couldn't even gather thirty mages from all across its lands, including those in branch families.

They didn't appear to notice me as I observed from above. I needed to take advantage of that. It was safe to assume that every one of the snake people rivaled my strength in close combat. Taking them all on would be suicide.

I'll wipe them all out with a surprise attack. I apologized to Nevan mentally. I was probably going to kill Naoise before delivering her message.

I used the force's current speed and direction to calculate their position ten minutes from now. I compared that to a memorized map of the kingdom and confirmed there were no settlements in that area. I was free to use one of my most devastating attacks.

"*Gungnir.*"

I formed a tungsten spear weighing one hundred kilograms and sent it up toward the heavens. By strength alone, this was the strongest spell I had. It used anti-gravity to lift a tungsten spear one thousand kilometers into the air and then let it free fall to annihilate the target with the force it picked up on the descent.

The spell was inspired by a weapon idea commonly known as "rods from God" in my previous world. The rods would have been dropped from space, achieving power that rivaled nuclear weapons upon impact. Technically, such a thing was possible, but the cost of placing heavy rods in space was prohibitive, so it was only ever done in tests. However, the reverse gravity spell allowed me to employ the deadly attack with a small amount of mana.

There were drawbacks, though. It took over ten minutes to land, and I couldn't adjust the impact point after firing the spear. Given this, it also required predicting the target's position. Achieving a direct hit in the middle of a fight was impossible.

Aiming was also extremely difficult, necessitating accurate environmental information and a complex calculation. It was more than achievable, however, with the advantages of magic and the brains of the smartest person alive—me. Furthermore, the orderly nature of Naoise's unit and its fixed travel pace made anticipating their future location easy.

"*Gungnir.*"

I released another god spear into the sky. The small mana cost enabled me to rapid-fire the spell.

"*Gungnir.*"

I sent yet another rod upward, and then two more. There were five in total, each with the power of a nuclear bomb. No matter how strong Naoise's group was, there was no way it could survive this.

I continued following Naoise's force from the sky, keeping my distance from the expected trajectory of the god spears. Even the impact aftermath was enough to kill me.

The spears would land in eighteen seconds. The knights were spurring on the snake monsters below me, still unaware that their lives were in mortal danger.

Then—impact. The first tungsten spear was too fast for eyes to follow as it descended. It didn't even make a sound when it landed. The ground ruptured, forming a crater multiple kilometers wide, and the shock waves dislodged everything in range. One spear changed the landscape forever.

The second, third, fourth, and fifth spears hit. The collisions kicked sediment into the air, blocking the sun on what had been a cloudless day. A tsunami of dirt sped outward in all directions, wiping out everything for dozens of kilometers. This was the level of destruction I could achieve with a concentrated fire of Gungnir. It was powerful enough to erase a city.

I watched until the dust finally cleared and the sun returned. My Tuatha Dé eyes, which could perceive mana, didn't catch a single sign of movement.

"A direct hit... The snake monsters are all dead. The knights, too."

The devastation I could cause with this magic was absurd. Each of those knights possessed strength on par with mine, but they died without getting a chance to use it. This could be considered the ultimate form of assassination.

I released the hang glider, used wind as a cushion to land, and inspected the crater formed by the god spears. It was a hellish pit with no visible bottom. The model version of this weapon from my previous world was said to be an environmentally friendly alternative to nuclear weapons, but I couldn't help but question that as I observed the destruction. There was no environment left.

"Naoise must be dead."

He should have been, anyway. I didn't think a demon's underling possessed their master's immortality. There was no way anything could have survived such a destructive barrage. My job was finished.

...Or not. I instinctively drew a knife to protect my neck, and a black-silver magic sword collided with it. The blade cut halfway through the knife, which was made of tough tungsten.

I responded with a spinning kick, knocking my assailant into the air and giving me some distance. Had I used a regular knife, the sword would have broken through it and severed my head. The very idea was enough to make me sweat.

"How cruel, Lugh. This is no way to treat a friend."

"I tried to kill you *because* you're my friend, Naoise. Let's end this."

I couldn't explain it, but somehow, Naoise stood before me. It didn't look like he dodged Gungnir; his armor and clothes were gone, leaving only his shining black sword. Becoming Mina's underling must have granted him some special ability. I needed to figure it out quickly, or I wouldn't be able to kill him.

One thing that interested me was that the black-silver magic sword he held wasn't as powerful as the pitch-black magic blade

I'd seen him wield before. This sword was incredible, but clearly inferior. The old one would have cut through my knife. Why wasn't he using it? The answer to that question would likely lead me to his secret.

"Oh, Lugh. You have the wrong idea. Do you think you're the ally of justice here?" Naoise sounded like a parent admonishing an ignorant child.

"I've never once fought for justice. I'm only acting in the best interest of the Alvanian Kingdom," I responded.

The Tuatha Dé clan's role was to remove presences harmful to the kingdom. While all the nobles I'd assassinated so far were villainous figures involved in illegal activities such as drug trafficking, slave trade, and thievery, I didn't kill them for justice. My family was a tool that protected the kingdom's best interests. Nothing more, nothing less. If my actions brought joy to those I cared about, that was enough for me.

"Give me a break. That's rich coming from the most beloved man in the realm. First a Holy Knight, then a saint. What's next? You can't tell me you're not killing demons for the glory. Now that I think about it, your presence is what threw my life off course. You stole all the praise that would have gone to me."

"That's possible. My actions allowed the government to keep Epona in the capital. There would've been no choice but to dispatch the hero otherwise. You might have made a name for yourself as Epona's assistant."

I took offense at Naoise's claim that I fought demons for prestige, but I couldn't deny that I had stolen opportunities from him.

"It's irrelevant now. I hate to break it to you, Lugh, but you've only made everything worse. *I* will be the one to exact justice. *I* am the only person who can. So don't get in my way. I'm ready to kill a friend for the sake of justice."

"...You keep using that word. Can you tell me what this justice of yours is?"

"Fine, if you insist. I'll enlighten you on the truth of the world."

He tried to act casual, but it was obvious how badly he wanted to lecture me. I was genuinely interested. Naoise massacred his own people and was about to do the same to another domain. What could legitimize that? What had Mina put into his head? Whatever she said was probably a lie to sway Naoise, but I had a feeling there was a kernel of truth I didn't know about.

Oblivious to my thoughts, Naoise began speaking with grand gestures as if he were the star in a play.

"First of all, demons were never our enemy," he said.

"You realize how many people demons kill, right? They've destroyed the academy and annihilated two cities—no, Geil makes that three. Yet you claim they're not the enemy?" I challenged.

"The destruction of a few cities is trivial in the grand scheme of things. Demons are a tool necessary for the world's survival, a device for correcting an overabundance of souls!"

I'd heard this somewhere before.

"Only a certain number of souls are supposed to exist in the world at once, yet that limit will inevitably be exceeded. When people die, their souls return to the world without being erased. That is why demons use Fruits of Life to reduce the number of souls."

That made sense. A dead person's soul went to heaven, where it was bleached and returned to the world. But making it part of a Fruit of Life removed the soul from the cycle of reincarnation, permanently destroying it.

"Huh, that's interesting. You said only a certain number of souls are supposed to exist. So what happens after the limit is surpassed?"

"The world collapses."

"Then why is there a hero? If demons exist to adjust the number of souls, the system shouldn't need a hero. They'd only get in the way."

"The Fruits of Life transform the victorious demon into the Demon King, who, if left unchecked, destroys too many souls. The hero's role is to kill the demons and the Demon King once their work is done. The fight between the hero and the Demon King ensures the world's survival."

"There has to be a less roundabout method."

That said, it was a good system. Demons were powerful beings that humans couldn't kill. They reduced the population, and in so doing, they killed each other in their competition to become the Demon King. That left a single Demon King for the hero to vanquish. It was a clean process.

"I thought the same thing, but Mistress Mina set me straight. She said that the system placed a burden on humanity to encourage them to grow. Humanity unites as one to defeat the demons, and they evolve in the process. Surely, you know how the fights against demons have pushed technology to progress."

That was new information, but Naoise was right. Humanity's need to oppose the demons led to advancements in military, medical, and distribution technology, to name a few. Improvements came quickest during wartime in my previous world as well. Naoise's assertion that the demon threat united people was correct, too. There was no time for squabbles while the enemy wreaked havoc across the continent. Undoubtedly, there'd be ongoing wars between nations if not for the threat of the demons. Considering the present international climate, it was surprising there wasn't a major war.

"Is that why you shackled yourself to a demon and sacrificed your people?"

"You have no idea how much it hurt my soul to kill my subjects. But someone has to do this, and I'm the only one who can! I dared to wonder if demons were truly the enemy, and that lack of prejudice led me to the truth. That's how I differ from you. You can't get over the idea that demons need to be eliminated. Only I am fit for this role."

"You realize that killing demons won't end the cycle."

"Naturally. It happens the same way every time. Demons appear, kill humans to make the Fruits of Life, one of them becomes the Demon King, and the hero kills them. How many thousands of years do you think humanity has gone through this foolish process? I'm going to end it once and for all."

"How?"

It was just as Naoise said—demons appeared, the Demon King was born, and the hero killed them. I'd read in history books that the cycle had repeated innumerable times. The waltz never ended.

"I'm going to make Mistress Mina into an invincible Demon King. She will conquer the world and become its overseer, culling the human population periodically to prevent the number of souls from climbing too high. My knights and I will perform that role for her. We'll kill people without worth and leave the elite."

"Ah, I see. That will remove the need for indiscriminate slaughter."

"Isn't it a great plan? We'll only kill those who deserve it. This world is full of worthless types, and we can end thousands of years of tragedy simply by rooting them out. There will be no need for a hero. I am the only necessary champion!"

Naoise couldn't hide his excitement. He even had a boner. He felt so good that he couldn't help it. It sounded as if he considered himself a god.

"How'd you like to enter my service, Lugh?" Naoise suggested.

"Now that takes me back. You asked me the same thing on the day of our entrance exams. I really was grateful. I don't have many guy friends," I responded.

I remembered it like yesterday. I found Naoise unpleasant at first, but I understood after talking to him that he was serious about his offer. He approached me because he recognized my talent.

"My feelings haven't changed. You should let Mistress Mina turn you into a monster so we can make the world a better place together. I'll forgive your insolence, and the way you looked down on me."

Naoise meant that in good faith. He truly thought he was doing the right thing. If everything Mina told him was true, then his plan did make a certain amount of sense.

"No, Naoise. You're not the same person you were then. I'm sorry, but I can't join you."

I readied my knife.

"Are you going to fight me?"

"No, I'm going to kill you."

That was my resolve. I wasn't fighting him as a friend—I was eliminating him as a noble assassin before he could do any more harm to the kingdom. I had already determined that Naoise was a lesion that needed to be removed. I was past forgiveness, or mercy, or sympathy. I was simply going to kill him. That was what I had decided.

I told Naoise I was going to kill him. There was no going back now. I observed him with my Tuatha Dé eyes and saw his mana building. He was ready to attack at any moment but still wore his usual friendly expression. Even as he prepared, he searched for a method other than killing me.

"You're a brilliant man, Lugh, but narrow-minded. I just gave you the whole picture, yet you still only think of Alvan. That's your weakness as a noble assassin."

"Didn't expect to hear you call me that."

It wasn't surprising that Naoise knew the Tuatha Dé were assassins. His mistress had worked her way into the center of the kingdom, and the four great dukedoms were always close to the royal family. The only people who were supposed to know of our secret were the royal family and House Romalung, who served as our direct bosses, but it had spread further.

"You've always kept me at a distance, despite our friendship. I wanted to hear the secret from you."

"That's just how we Tuatha Dé are. No assassin worth his salt gives himself away."

"Is it more important than our friendship?"

"They're not comparable. That's like a woman asking her man if he thinks his job is more important than her," I joked.

I entertained Naoise's conversation while looking for an opportunity to strike, although it was also partly due to a personal weakness. I wanted to stretch this out as long as I could.

"Ah-ha-ha, that is certainly annoying. Well, you may be ready to kill me, but I haven't given up yet."

"You're telling me to sell my soul to a demon as you did?"

"Yes. I know you see the logic, Lugh. The world will be destroyed if the number of souls climbs too high. Killing demons to protect people is pointless. How do you know the next round of demons won't appear immediately after you finish this one?"

He sounded like a parent reasoning with an unruly child.

"It's possible. And everything we've done will be for nothing if the world crumbles because of too many souls."

"As a noble assassin, you should understand the danger of fixating on the short-term benefit. Quit playing at justice and join me in saving the people who deserve to live. Or are you addicted to the praise?"

"Don't make me repeat myself. I'm an assassin—I couldn't care less about accolades. I only serve as the kingdom's shadow and wield my blade for its benefit."

The desire to become a hero was innate, and I was no exception. Everyone craves fame and attention. But I was reincarnated into this world to save it and reared as a blade to safeguard national interest. I needed to prioritize country over any desire for recognition. I felt like I had done a fine job at that.

"Then you should join me. There will be many benefits. I'll share with you the privilege of choosing who to sacrifice. That way you can ensure you won't lose those you love. And if you hold that much pride in your role as the Alvanian Kingdom's blade, we can cull populations abroad. You'll be able to protect national interest however you like."

That was an attractive proposal. I could protect my beloved Tuatha Dé domain, Milteu, and most importantly, my family and fiancées. I was no philanthropist. You wouldn't hear me preaching that all lives are equal. If I was asked to choose to save someone I'd never heard of and someone I cared about, I would pick the latter immediately.

"I only have one hang-up. I love the Tuatha Dé domain with all my heart. It's why your proposal tempted me for a moment. However, you're the heir to a domain like I am. What made you able to sacrifice the people you loved?"

"Hah, the strength of my conviction. If I am going to thin the human populace, I need to know the pain I'll put others through. Killing my beloved citizens will prepare me to command others to die for the sake of the world."

He looked at me with a determined gaze, trying and failing to hide his sadness, just like the protagonist of a tragedy. His handsome features made him look picturesque in his pain.

"How absurd. You disgrace yourself, Naoise." I voiced the first thought that came to my mind. Veins bulged in Naoise's temple.

"There are certain things you shouldn't say to a friend. Don't you dare belittle my conviction. Do you know how much I suffered over this?! How much I wept?! You can't possibly understand how hard it is to kill your own people!" he screamed.

"You think this is self-sacrifice, but you're off the mark. The people of the Gephis domain bear the pain of this incident, not you."

"I *know* my people are hurting. That's exactly why this is so hard for me!" Naoise screamed, but I didn't back down. As an heir myself, I couldn't budge on this.

"Let me be clear. You're nothing but a murderer… Your people are not yours to offer up. Nobles must protect the people and land entrusted to them. Losing sight of that fundamental truth is why you murdered innocents while believing you're some tragic figure. Once again—they're the victims. Not you."

We nobles guided our people, protected them, and gave them comfortable lives in exchange for taxes. Nobles and their subjects had an equivalent relationship. They weren't our property.

"I know! Yet I still drew my sword against them. I needed to know the agony I will inflict."

This was sad. My words weren't getting through to him.

"Your tragic act after massacring innocents proves you understand nothing… I feel bad for the people of Gephis for being saddled with such a clueless heir."

"Shut up."

"I won't. Why did you believe the words of a demon so easily, anyway? Their kind is the enemy of humanity. Mina probably lied to you. Did you make any effort to verify her claim that the world will collapse under the weight of its souls?"

I always verified the information I received. Data was more valuable than gold in the criminal underworld, which led to a lot of falsification.

"I told you to shut up!"

"I won't. I think Mina fooled you into thinking you're saving the world, when in reality, you just butchered thousands for her."

"No. No, I refuse to believe it. I—I became a true hero. I surpassed you!"

"And out slips your true motive. You talk about saving the

world, self-sacrifice, and your conviction, but all you really wanted was fame. The world couldn't matter less to you. You just couldn't stand feeling inferior to me."

"SHUT UUUUUUUUP!"

Naoise extended his right hand, transforming it into a serpent that raced toward me faster than a bullet... But he was interrupted when his head was blasted off his shoulders, causing the snake to fall limp before it reached me. I'd sniped him.

"Sorry, but I'm an assassin. This is the only way I can fight."

Once I confirmed that Naoise had survived Gungnir, I camouflaged multiple cannons and fixed them into the ground nearby. I controlled them remotely with magic. I couldn't adjust their aim, but I could lure Naoise into their line of fire. I'd never fight fair against an enemy empowered by a demon to the point that he could survive a direct hit from Gungnir. I was an assassin, not a knight. Aesthetics and pride meant nothing to me in a fight. I simply killed.

That said, I couldn't relax just because I'd cut off his head.

"Gun Strike."

I drew my gun and shot the headless Naoise. This was a new gun I'd made for this mission; I didn't trust my usual one to be powerful enough. The model was the same—a Pfeifer Zeliska, said to be the strongest revolver in my former world—and I'd made some modifications. The Pfeifer Zeliska ditched the portability and adaptability that handguns provided in favor of greater size and firepower. I used .600 Nitro Express rounds. They were typically used with rifles and were made for hunting large animals like elephants and buffalo, not humans. The result made the Desert Eagle, a powerful and famous pistol, look like a toy.

The formidable bullets were made even stronger because I packed them with Fahr Stone powder, which was significantly more explosive than gunpowder. Additionally, I used tungsten for the warheads to make them more penetrative. The recoil was so strong that my ribs would've shattered were I not strengthened with mana. It was a flawed gun that prioritized strength over everything else, but I didn't want it any other way.

"...Sorry, Naoise."

I fired until the barrel was empty, blowing a several-dozen-centimeters-wide hole in the ground. There wasn't a trace of Naoise's body left, yet I kept on guard. I used a wind spell to probe the area while quickly reloading. I didn't trust for a second that this was the end of Naoise. If this were enough to kill him, Gungnir would have done the trick. I still didn't know how he survived.

"Tch."

I felt a small vibration under my feet. My probing spell hadn't picked up anything, but I trusted my instinct and jumped. Immediately after, a white snake emerged from the ground and sped for me. That explained why I didn't sense it—the wind probing spell couldn't locate anything underground.

I couldn't dodge, so I protected my vital points. The snake changed its trajectory without slowing and slammed into my open stomach, producing a dull *crunch*. That was the sound of my bulletproof vest being overloaded and breaking to absorb the impact, but it was unable to diffuse the entire attack, and I was sent flying.

That snake's attack was as strong as a blow from Epona... One strike broke my jacket, which was resilient enough to withstand a hit from a truck. My ribs and organs would've been pulverized without it. I was right to repair it.

I rolled upon landing to lessen the impact, then looked around.

Another snake burst from the ground, and then two more. The first charged at me from the front, and the others came from each flank. I quickly jumped backward and pushed myself with wind for greater speed, putting all three snakes in front of me. Then I threw a Fahr Stone engineered to create a directional explosion. The bomb blast and iron scraps flew forward, killing all three snakes.

I used wind magic to float and avoid any more surprise attacks.

"I know you're still alive, Naoise. Come on out."

Naoise emerged from underground in response.

"I'm surprised. I didn't think a human would survive. Almost makes me suspect you're a second hero," he said.

"I'm just human, unfortunately. I try to make up for it with ingenuity," I responded.

I observed Naoise. He was wearing different equipment than before. His armor set was an heirloom of House Gephis. Maha had included it in the list she put together of all known divine treasures. According to legend, it had survived over a hundred battles without a scratch. At his hip, Naoise wore a familiar black magic sword. *So that's why he was using the weaker weapon earlier.*

"The Naoise I just killed was a fake," I said.

"No, both versions you have killed were genuine. I suppose there's no harm in giving away the trick. There were three of me. Snakes rule over rebirth and immortality. Mistress Mina gifted me with two special snakes that assumed my form, and both became a full extension of me. Only one of my three bodies can move at a time. If one dies, another version of me, sleeping in the estate, wakes up and switches places with them. Impressive, no?"

I knew Mina had given him power, but I never thought he'd strayed this far from humanity.

"You shouldn't have told me that."

I used the wind holding me in the air to descend quickly. More snake monsters burst from the ground around Naoise. They must have been outside the range of the god spears, coming here after I destroyed Naoise's force. Three of the serpents flung themselves at me like spears as I approached from the sky. I took position to hit Naoise and the snake monsters, throwing multiple Fahr Stones adjusted to produce directional explosions. They burst violently and pummeled my targets with iron scraps, but unlike before, the serpents moved through unharmed.

I studied them closely and noticed that their scales shone like gold. They were a new variety.

"Tch."

I shot down two snakes with my handgun, used the recoil to dodge the third, and dropped it once I landed. *So they can survive a Fahr Stone explosion, but not being pierced by a large-caliber bullet.*

As the dust cleared, I looked toward Naoise. A giant snake was coiled around him, presumably for protection. That explained how he survived the Fahr Stone blast. Iron scraps had pierced the snake's charred skin, but none of the injuries were lethal. This serpent was absurdly tough. It uncoiled and allowed Naoise to step free.

"Whew, someone's in a violent mood. I don't have any more spares, you know. That actually might've killed me."

I attached a long barrel to my handgun to turn it into a rifle and fired four times. His snake monsters took the hits for him.

"It's no use, Lugh. These monsters are special. Their scales are as hard as orichalcum. I know you want to kill me from a distance like an assassin, but it's not going to happen… Let's fight as proper nobles! Proper knights!"

Naoise charged. He was fast—I didn't have time to cast my flying spell. I threw a Fahr Stone to stop him, but he raced past it, and the stone exploded behind him. He then drew the black sword and stabbed at me. Unable to dodge, I blocked his thrust with my handgun, unfortunately breaking it, but that afforded me the chance to kick Naoise in the temple.

The soles and tips of my boots were plated with metal for defensive and offensive purposes. Nevan began using metal-plated shoes after seeing me use these. A full-strength kick with the metal tip could easily break someone's skull.

My boot connected with Naoise's head with a *clang* like metal on metal. That's when I realized his skin was blanketed with tightly packed scales. This didn't stop me, though. I couldn't hurt him, but I could knock him off-balance. I followed up by slashing Naoise with a large knife strapped to my thigh, but he parried with his sword.

Unsurprisingly, I wasn't strong enough to defeat Naoise and his newfound demon powers in a straight fight. I needed distance, but Naoise moved faster than I could retreat. Left with no alternative, I traded blows with him like he wanted.

"I know the assassin in you must be fuming!" Naoise taunted between heavy breaths. He looked to be having the time of his life as he brandished his weapon. I defended myself silently. "You don't have the opportunity for any cheap tricks or magic. Knights hold the advantage in close quarters!"

I'd been trained as a knight, but it wasn't my specialty. Naoise definitely had the upper hand at this range.

His attacks turned more ferocious. The old Naoise would have been fatigued at this pace and given me a chance to attack, but he showed no sign of slowing down. Instead, I struggled to keep up despite my massively superior stamina. He was so fast that I only barely had time to defend.

"So you can handle yourself at a knight's distance, assassin! I'm impressed by your skill."

I needed to break out of this deadlock, but I couldn't figure out how. Letting Naoise get this close with his physical advantage was a lethal mistake. No matter how many cards I had up my sleeve, they were useless if I couldn't find the time or space to use them. *He's strong, fast, and skilled. This is harder to deal with than any special ability Mina gave him.*

The only way to endure Naoise's assault was to give up attacking and focus solely on guarding. And frustratingly, he wouldn't go for a killing blow. He thought only of preventing me from moving away, an attempt to wear me out that banked on him winning because of this physical advantage. The way he ignored all my attempts to bait him into trying to finish me was proof of that. I'd only be able to withdraw if he got impatient.

At this rate, I was bound to lose. If he wouldn't take a gamble, then I had no choice but to try one.

"...Reconsider, Naoise," I implored.

"Cut the crap, Lugh. You said you were going to kill me."

"You can still rejoin society."

"It's too late. I'd be executed as a traitor if I surrendered now... Getting killed earlier cooled my head and helped me realize that it doesn't matter whether or not Mistress Mina told me the truth. It'll become the truth once she conquers the world."

Naoise wouldn't budge. Nothing I said reached him. *I suppose he's standing his ground.* He was right that history was written by the victors—if Mina ruled, her word would be truth.

"It's time for you to die for the cause."

He cut my knife in two with his black sword and scraped my face, leaving a shallow wound that bled heavily. I jumped back with all my strength, but he caught up immediately. I'd been deflecting Naoise's black sword at an angle because I knew it would break my dagger if I tried to block it head-on, but fatigue slowed my reaction, and my clumsy retreat only exposed me further... Or at least, that was what I wanted Naoise to think.

This was my gamble. I purposefully left myself vulnerable so Naoise would attack. I'd been doing the same thing since he engaged me at close range, but a swordsman as good as Naoise could tell when an opening was fake. This time I made myself truly vulnerable—I actually wouldn't be able to dodge his next blow.

Naoise loosed a diagonal slash. *Finally, the large swing I've been waiting for.* His blade was headed for my left shoulder. Given Naoise's skill and the sharpness of the black sword, I had no doubt the weapon would cut through armor. I rushed forward while watching the blade from the corner of my eye.

"Are you planning on sacrificing yourself to take me out? You're too predictable." A shining gold snake coiled around Naoise's armor.

His sword landed on my left shoulder. I wore the same stab-proof clothes I'd made for Dia and Tarte. The robust fabric blocked his blade, but it couldn't eliminate the impact, and my shoulder broke with a dull sound. I did my best to bear the intense pain while rushing forward. Using mana, I forced my broken left arm forward, a sluggish and weakened movement.

"You're wasting effort," he taunted.

That would have been true if I were trying to strike him directly. I had no chance of piercing the snake monster and his divine treasure, but I had a plan. I was holding a Fahr Stone in my left hand engineered to produce a directional explosion, and it overloaded and ruptured as I opened my fist. My left arm was already broken, so it hardly mattered if I injured it worse.

The explosion sent Naoise and me flying in opposite directions. While the stone was configured to give Naoise the brunt of the blast, I couldn't protect myself from taking some amount of damage. My left arm was horribly burned from the elbow down. I also suffered a compound fracture, and my shoulder was still broken from Naoise's attack. Rapid Recovery couldn't mend this on its own. The arm would be useless for the rest of the fight.

However, my sacrifice won me some distance and managed to injure Naoise, too. Not even his divine treasure armor and scales could fully protect him from a point-blank blast. The heat scorched his body, and the sound and shock wave injured his sensory organs.

This was well worth sacrificing my left arm.

I stood and studied Naoise carefully. His eyes were burned, his nose was misshapen, and his eardrums had ruptured. Now I could use any weapon I liked. My next attack would definitely connect. This would be my first and last chance to kill him. The same plan wouldn't work twice.

I need the firepower to break through his armor and the snake scales. Gungnir could have done it, but that required ten minutes to land. My next most powerful attack, Railgun, demanded half a minute of preparation, which was still too long.

Naoise's burned face was healing quickly. His senses would return soon. I needed something strong and swift. A Fahr Stone with a directional explosion lacked the strength to kill him, and the same was true of Cannon Volley. Fortunately, I knew just the thing.

I'm basing this on Dia's attack on the earth dragon demon. It utilized dozens of Fahr Stones positioned to force the blasts inward, crushing the enemy to death. In my previous world, weapons that used this technique were called cluster bombs. I created magic systemizing the process that normally required careful calculations and a precise combination of spells, and produced a special weapon to use it with.

"Cluster Bombing."

I retrieved the weapon I produced for a spell I called Cluster Bombing from my Leather Crane Bag and threw it. It was shaped like a coconut and contained cushioning, gunpowder, and twenty special small Fahr Stones within its iron coating. Magic carried it above Naoise's head, and that's when the first blast went off. It wasn't from the Fahr Stones but from the weakened gunpowder. The iron coating broke, scattering the Fahr Stones around Naoise in midair. They were in the ideal positions to concentrate force toward the center.

The small Fahr Stones reached their capacities and ruptured simultaneously, trapping the impact and heat of the explosions where Naoise stood. The result was a giant sphere that resembled the sun. It consumed the ground beneath.

"This is Cluster Bombing, a spell that weaponizes Dia's sophisticated calculations... It's the strongest attack I can use in direct combat."

Cluster Bombing's operating theory was simple. The shock waves and heat from explosions traveled outward radially. So a single target only received a small fraction of the total force.

But what would happen if you positioned countless small bombs around the target and triggered them all at once? The heat and shock waves hammered the target from all sides, crushing them. This resulted in eight times more force than simply scattering bombs at random. Naoise was struck with octuple the power of twenty Fahr Stones. No living creature could endure that.

"Sorry, Naoise. I didn't want to kill you, but I made up my mind."

Even if everything Mina put in Naoise's head was true, I couldn't join in culling the human population. I would find another method.

Naoise only survived Gungnir because he used a duplicate, and if he spoke the truth, there were only two of them. Now he was dead for good. I exhaled and began stowing my equipment...

"Gah..."

...and that's when a black sword sprouted from my chest.

"You were really dumb enough to believe me? I actually had three duplicates. I decided to follow your example and pull a little trick to get you to drop your guard after you killed me the third time. Only a fool would give away something that important."

Naoise was behind me. *I see. He gave away his secret to surprise me on the off chance I managed to kill him again.*

"I figured you were planning something like that."

I—or rather, my projection—laughed. My form then warped and melted, turning into a simple clump of metal.

"Wh-what?! My sword...is stuck...!" Naoise tried to force his blade free, but iron bars grew from the ground and formed a cage around him.

He should have expected this. There was no way I'd trust Naoise after lecturing him on the foolishness of trusting a demon.

I doubted his claim immediately and set up a trap, knowing he planned to ambush me when I killed his third double. The moment I slew the final body double, I produced a metal doll in the cloud of dust that my attack kicked up, then retreated and used a light-bending spell to project my image onto the facsimile.

The true ace up my sleeve descended upon Naoise from above—Gungnir. I couldn't hit a moving enemy, but it was easy to set a decoy and aim for that. I launched the spear into the air as insurance, figuring it wouldn't be a big deal if it missed.

The god spear slammed into the ground at dozens of times the speed of sound, launching a tsunami of dirt in all directions and carving a crater hundreds of meters wide.

"Deceit is the domain of assassins. You should have known better, Naoise... You lost sight of who I am."

Naoise was truly dead this time. His mistake was not sticking to his specialty of fighting like a knight. Had he not played my game, he could have won. Actually, his error came long before—when he accepted Mina's power. And that wouldn't have happened if not for me. Naoise's sense of inferiority allowed that snake demon to take advantage of him.

"Am I...crying?"

I had no right to cry over this. I wiped the tears. There was still something I needed to do, a task so important I killed a friend for it. There was no way I could stop now. I wouldn't forgive myself.

I forced my aching body to walk.

Epilogue

After using every probing and analysis spell I had to scan the area and eliminate any possibility that Naoise survived, I returned to the Gephis domain. Epona had successfully pulled Mina away from the city of Geil, and they were still fighting elsewhere. Magic knights employed by House Romalung marched into the city, wiping out the monsters. I heard that Dia and Tarte accompanied and fought with them. Naoise leading most of the Gephis-troops-turned-snake-people away undoubtedly helped the Romalung forces triumph. The enemy would have been too strong otherwise.

I visited the strategic headquarters set up by the knights to report the details of Naoise's plan and that I'd killed him and his followers. Then I went to an infirmary.

"I need to treat my left arm."

The limb throbbed in agony from injuries I inflicted on myself to trap Naoise. Rapid Recovery only sped up the natural healing process and didn't work on wounds that couldn't mend on their own. The left shoulder fracture from Naoise's sword would heal fine, but the heavy burns and compound break the Fahr Stone explosion left would never improve without treatment.

Instead of trusting the doctors on hand, I intended to deal with the injuries myself. None of them could beat my Tuatha Dé medical knowledge.

I readied myself and summoned my artificial arm divine treasure. First, I removed my broken bones and produced metal with magic to reinforce and shape the remaining ones. Next, I tore off my burned and dead skin and implanted living tissue removed from elsewhere on my body. Magic and Rapid Recovery made this possible. Once I completed the basic treatment, I wrapped my arm with special tape and created a metal cast to hold the snapped bones in place and protect them.

Rapid Recovery would handle the rest, likely requiring three days. Unfortunately, the arm would never truly be as it was before.

"Lugh! I heard you were seriously injured!"

"Are you okay, my lord?!"

Dia and Tarte ran into the infirmary covered in mud and dust.

"There's no need to worry. It was just my left arm, and I've already treated it."

"Thank goodness. Everyone was freaking out about your injury when we got here. It scared me," Dia said.

Tarte frowned. "I knew I should have gone with you."

Dia hugged me, and Tarte teared up. The sight of them eased my tension somewhat.

"I was worried about you two as well. The Gephis knights were really strong. I'm glad you're all right," I responded.

"Forget about us. You're in much worse shape."

"Yes. Please leave matters to everyone else and get some rest."

I tried to stand, but they pushed me back into bed.

"...Let me go. I need to leave after an hour of rest. I want to get ready," I protested.

"What are you planning to do in your state?" Dia questioned.

"Help Epona against the snake demon. They're still fighting."

Any battle involving Epona meant destruction on the scale of a natural disaster. She and Mina were fighting far from the city, but the sounds, light, and heat of the struggle were perceptible from here. No knights could help, no matter how elite they were. Mina seemed Epona's equal in strength now that she'd consumed a Fruit of Life. I couldn't beat her alone, but I could tip the scale by supporting Epona.

"Don't be absurd! Trust Epona and stay put. You'd only be a burden like this."

"That's right. No one can heal a broken arm that quickly. Not even you, my lord. And I can tell that you've exhausted your mana."

They were both deeply concerned, and honestly, they were also correct.

"That's why I'm going to rest for an hour. That's enough time for my wound to close and for me to regain some energy."

My broken bones needed a few days to heal, but they were safe in a cast. Thanks to the skin graft, the wound would close, and the pain from the burns lessened with every passing moment.

Dia sighed. "We're not stopping you. I see it on your face."

"I want to know if Naoise was right, or if he was deceived… And most importantly, I need to make Mina pay," I declared.

Killing Naoise was my crime, but she was the one who forced me to it.

"Okay. Fine. But you have to take us with you."

"We've gotten stronger. We won't get in the way."

"Do you realize what you're volunteering for? This is a battle between Epona and a demon who has taken a step toward becoming the Demon King. It will be dangerous, even for you two."

"Trust me, I'm scared. But I've made up my mind."

"We'll make up for the injury to your left arm."

I could tell from the looks in their eyes that they were determined, no matter what I said. They would probably follow me if

I tried to leave them behind. And that was much more dangerous than allowing the pair to tag along.

Hold on, I have a better solution.

"...Dia, Tarte, why do you two look ready to fight me?"

They eyed me warily, as if expecting me to attack them. I didn't stand a chance of getting a hit in—if I tried, they'd undoubtedly get the best of me, given my fatigue and the state of my left arm.

"Because we know you. You're thinking of knocking us out and then leaving without us."

"Lady Dia's right. You can render us unconscious with one blow to the chin. We wouldn't be able to stand for three hours."

"Right? One pop, and the whole world is spinning. It's terrifying."

They saw through me. I shouldn't have used that trick on them before.

"Fine. You win. Let's go together," I conceded.

Dia grinned. "That's what I wanted to hear."

"I'll get our equipment," Tarte announced.

Dia sat on my bed while Tarte rushed out of the infirmary. Tarte went to get our things alone so Dia could keep an eye on me. It was no use trying to stop them, so I reached for my desk, grabbing a pouch full of nutritional fluid. I emptied it and ate the rest of my preserved food. When finished, I lay down, hoping to sleep and recover as best I could.

Dia patted my head.

"Why are you doing that?"

"Because you seem sad. You look like you could cry, Lugh," Dia said.

"I killed a friend. Of course I'm sad. There was no other

choice, and I thought I'd made peace with my decision… But I guess not."

I killed countless friends in my past life. On orders from my organization, I eliminated any who betrayed us. These were necessary deeds, and I felt nothing committing them. Those people were mere tools. The current version of me could never behave that way.

"It's natural to be sad. I know that was hard for you, Lugh."

Dia stroked my head again. I felt my grief wane, but I felt guilty for it.

"Rest. I'll stay by your side."

"…Thank you. That's a real comfort."

I closed my eyes to the warmth of Dia's body heat. I'd force Mina to confess everything. Then I'd kill her. Such was my duty as a noble assassin. My job was to remove all threats to the kingdom, but this time…I truly hated my target.

Afterword

Thank you very much for reading *The World's Finest Assassin Gets Reincarnated in Another World as an Aristocrat*, Vol. 7.

I'm Rui Tsukiyo, the author.

This volume focuses on Lugh's fight against his friend. I hope you paid attention to Lugh's emotions as you read. He demonstrated his humanity more this time than in any previous books.

Changing the topic, season one of the anime finished broadcasting. It's no exaggeration to say it was very popular. I was surprised by the response. I'm working hard on the novels so the show can continue.

Thank you for being so supportive, everyone! Anyone who hasn't seen the anime should check out the various streaming sites where it's available.

Unfortunately, I have not been feeling well of late. I began to suffer from some depression while the anime was airing. I was recovering with the help of a prescription, but sometime after the anime finished, my doctor said that I'd healed and changed my medication to something weaker. That was a trap.

As soon as I started the weaker medicine, I became unable to look at emails and social media, fearing other people's opinions. Fortunately, after lessening my treatment in increments, I have completely healed (my doctor has given their approval). I don't need the prescription anymore!

I'm grateful for that, but I didn't look at emails or social media while I was recovering. It wasn't a great situation.

As a result, I ended up wholly estranged from all my work relationships over the last year.

But as I said before, my health is gradually improving, so I'm going to do my best to hit my stride as an author again!

Thanks

To Reia, thank you for your wonderful illustrations!

To the editing team and all involved at Kadokawa Sneaker Bunko; the lead designer, Takahisa Atsuji; and all the people who have read this far, thank you very much!

The World's Finest Assassin Gets Reincarnated in Another World as an Aristocrat, Vol. 7

((I am speaking directly into your brain... Watch the anime version of *The World's Finest Assassin*... It's super cool! I promise!))

The character designs are so cute!!

HAVE YOU BEEN TURNED ON TO LIGHT NOVELS YET?

86—EIGHTY-SIX, VOL. 1-11

In truth, there is no such thing as a bloodless war. Beyond the fortified walls protecting the eighty-five Republic Sectors lies the "nonexistent" Eighty-Sixth Sector. The young men and women of this forsaken land are branded the Eighty-Six and, stripped of their humanity, pilot "unmanned" weapons into battle...

Manga adaptation available now!

WOLF & PARCHMENT, VOL. 1-6

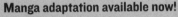

The young man Col dreams of one day joining the holy clergy and departs on a journey from the bathhouse, Spice and Wolf. Winfiel Kingdom's prince has invited him to help correct the sins of the Church. But as his travels begin, Col discovers in his luggage a young girl with a wolf's ears and tail named Myuri, who stowed away for the ride!

Manga adaptation available now!

SOLO LEVELING, VOL. 1-8

E-rank hunter Jinwoo Sung has no money, no talent, and no prospects to speak of—and apparently, no luck, either! When he enters a hidden double dungeon one fateful day, he's abandoned by his party and left to die at the hands of some of the most horrific monsters he's ever encountered.

Comic adaptation available now!